THE SY

by Mark Cunnington

Trio Publishing

First published 1999

Second edition 2000

Published by Trio Publishing
50 Gillsman's Park
St. Leonards-on-Sea
East Sussex
TN38 0SW

ISBN 0 9537951 0 1

Copyright © Mark Cunnington 1999, 2000

All rights reserved. No part of this publication may be reproduced, stored or introduced into any type of retrieval system, or transmitted, in any form, or by any means without the prior written permission of the publisher.

This book is sold subject to the condition that it shall not, by way of trade or otherwise, be lent, re-sold, hired out or otherwise circulated without the publisher's prior consent in any form of binding or cover other than in which it is published and without a similar condition including this condition being imposed on the subsequent purchaser.

Printed and bound by Chandlers Printers Ltd
Bexhill-on-Sea, East Sussex

INTRODUCTION

I guess in the beginning we were much like any of the hundreds of carp fishing syndicates up and down the country. Just a small group of enthusiastic individuals who had achieved the ambition to run and own a small lake for the benefit of like minded fishermen. Our own little angling Mecca, to do, within reason, as we pleased and in whatever manner suited us. An ideal scenario you may think, perfect in every detail . . . If only life lived up to expectations and reality mirrored dreams it would be . . . well, it would be a lot better than the way life is for me at the moment. But I must not turn bitter, older hands tell me bitterness eats away at you. If you are to survive in this God forsaken place that I find myself you must be mellow and go with the flow. Survive in the mind they say, it has no locked doors, no barriers, it is free to roam wherever it pleases, unlike myself. I digress, so, this is my tale that I have more than ample time to tell. It is a tale of caution, a warning of the human condition that affects us all, although we may well deny it. Above all it is a story of mistake after mistake, of missed takes, of drop backs and bollocks dropped, belting runs and scheming scum, bad behaviour and secret flavour, protein mix and clever dicks, the smug and sure with the insecure, expensive tackle and loads of hassle, of dreams turning to nightmares.

Chapter 1

The syndicate had been up and running for about six years. There had been an initial turnover of members as some fell by the wayside due to work commitments, family, lack of success and so on but the last couple of seasons had seen the ten members settle down into a fairly harmonious group. There were disagreements as there are within any group of people, but on the whole things looked very rosy for the S.S (Southern Specimens) as we had so humorously named ourselves. (We had thought the name to be enigmatic and ambiguous. Did it refer to the fish, to the members or to something quite different? Of course this was without its Nazi connections that the initials so blatantly conjured up. For the uninformed this was all they actually could relate to as we had never banded around what they stood for. Tradders said that it reflected on the fact that we were a pompous bunch of tossers but as he said it some three years after it had been voted upon and passed, being a later member, this made little difference. Tom had smugly informed him the only thing remotely fascist about the S.S was the stance he used when weighing a fish with scales and a weigh sling. This apparently vaguely mimicked the Gestapo salute only Tom used two hands because the fish were invariably so hefty.)

Our 3 acre lake was in good condition and was as pretty as a picture, much the same could be said for the carp that were in it but definitely not for the ten oiks that fished it. Six seasons had passed and the efforts of work parties had transformed the original weed choked, bramble lined lake into a thing of beauty. The initial expense of purchasing 100 six to eight pound carp of good strain was paying dividends, we now had ten different twenties that we knew of and loads of high doubles. In 1992, six years into our ownership things were great. Once again 100% turn out work parties had prepared the water for the glorious 16th so it was with some trepidation and excitement that the ten of us met above the 'Black Horse' for the draw for swims for the opening night. It is from here that my tale really begins, from the close season of that year. I shall tell you my story as it happened to the best of my ability and attempt to keep hindsight to a minimum and not let acerbity spoil the taste of my memories. Fat chance!

I entered the empty public bar and ordered a pint from the landlord. "You're late Matt, all the others are up there," he raised his eyes upward.

"Yeah, I know. I expect I'll get some stick for making them wait." I took my drink and went through the door that led to the dingy stairs which in turn led to the small room that had served as our S.S HQ ever since the syndicate had been started by Tom Watt, Ya Man himself and Kipper Cole. The bi-monthly meetings, AGMs and first day draws all took place in the room above the public bar of the 'Black Horse'. It was a part of the syndicate and as I swung open the door 18 eyes of another part of the syndicate focused on me. The members. At that moment I could probably say with all honesty that I got on with all of them. Ha ha! How time changes everything.

"Good of you to turn up, Williams. You've been scratched from the draw. We didn't think you'd mind, seeing as you probably won't catch anything in any case." The room rippled with laughter.

"Thanks, Tom, but my money's as good as yours so just reinstate me, ok?" I said with as much wit and humour as possible. The truth can be tricky to face up to.

"All right then." Tom gave me a friendly smile that lacked warmth and friendship come to that. I was not one of Tom's clique. Tom was the most successful angler on the syndicate water and pretty nearly every other water that he fished on. He was good. He knew he was good and even worse he knew that we knew that he was good. Tom was happiest talking about fishing and catching fish, he was even happier when he was talking about himself fishing and catching fish. He was clever enough to be arrogant in a humble way, a trick managed by few.

"Now then gentlemen, now that we are all here," Tom smiled pointedly at me again as I sat down next to Dave and Tony, "we shall start." Tom sat behind a table with Kipper, the backs of their chairs pinched tight against the wall. The table separated the two of them from the rest of us, the other eight, as it used to register in my mind. These two were our founders. Yoh Respect!

Tom continued. "Firstly I would like to thank you all for the excellent days work we had in May. I think you'll agree that the effort we have all put in is now being repaid manifold. We have a super water, super fish and four years left on our lease, which as you know we have first option on forever. Our insistence of the option being written in as a covenant on the deeds to the farm has insured our future for as long as we can come up with the money. The cost of each ten year lease will be linked to inflation. We will not be gazumped by another group of band wagon jumpers. In short we are lucky men."

A few stifled 'here here's' went around the room along with a murmur of approval. It was all sewn up. It had been all sewn up from the time Tom had negotiated with the farmer on whose land our little bit of paradise resided six years ago. Tom just wanted us to be reminded of his great work.

"We are lucky men, but tonight some will be luckier than others. Gentlemen the draw." Excited eyes met across the sparsely lit room, several rueful grins spread across gleaming faces. Next to me I saw Tony cross his fingers and tuck them between the thighs of his crossed legs. A few hopes would aspire tonight, a few would be dashed.

"I have ten pieces of paper with your individual names written on them, in the bag that Kipper has are ten ping-pong balls numbered from 1 to 10. I will choose a name at random and then one of you will pick a ball from the bag. Thus the swims will be allocated to each member. To refresh your memories swim number one is The Oak, two - Little Pads, three - Wide Swim, four - The Island, five - The Deep Corner, six - Big Pads, seven - The Pines, eight - First Twenty, nine and ten are The Bay East and West."

Tom let his words sink in to the anxious souls that were bared before him. A quick straw poll would have seen most members willing to donate their wife, girlfriend or life savings for a chance to fish either the Island or the Big Pads. They always produced first week, you could bet on it, the others were not so hot. Six years of fair pressure was beginning to make the water get a little harder. Maybe a bit stupidly our fish had been subjected to hair rigs and heavy fixed leads from the onset and things were getting a bit tighter and we had few places left to run. Well, us ordinary mortals felt that we had nowhere to run, others seem to have the world in front of them.

Tom smiled benignly. "Ok. Ahm . . . Mike, would you do the honours for the swims?"

"No probs." Mike walked up to the table. Mike and Tom were much like the fingers between Tony's thighs, like that. Add Harry and you had the big three, the clique, the knot. They were the three that talked together on the bank and stopped when you came by to say hello. As soon as you left they started again. They were the three that caught, the three that fished the circuit waters, the three that went in on bait together, they were friendly but told you nothing. If by some fluke you happened to be the one who was having success they would come around and be very nice. So exalted did you feel that they should grace you with their presence that you normally ended up telling them everything although you vowed you wouldn't. I guess with hindsight I can see all that, at the time it never really registered until, well, more of that later.

"The first name is, Brian Kipper Cole." Tom smiled at his co-founder who excitedly thrust the bag at Mike. Mike rummaged in the bag and pulled out a ball. "Number three, Wide Swim." Kipper barely managed to hide his disappointment, not a good draw.

"Plenty of shut-eye there old mate," said Mike laughing. Brian's nickname had nothing to do with big fish. Here was a man who, when coupled with a bedchair, achieved instant horizontal harmony, he could easily out sleep Rip Van Winkle.

Mike called out another name. "Second name is Alan Buck. Good luck, Tencher ...... you will fish number two, the Little Pads." Alan nodded with enthusiasm, his main quarry were the tench that had grown to six pounds plus no doubt on a diet of good quality boilies. Pads and tench were good news for him.

The draw continued, Tradders got First Twenty so called for the obvious but not a well liked swim generally. Rambo got the Bay East and the I got the Bay West. This could be a bit hit and miss for the pair of us as the bay was right up the north end of the lake and the fish were either up there or they weren't. Now that may sound like stating the obvious, but it wasn't an area that the fish seemed to patrol through, even in summer you could sit up the bay and not see a carp for days.

Tension was mounting for the five members that were left, especially as the two best swims were still in the bag. Then it happened, Ya Man Tom Watt pulled the Island, the jammy bastard.

"Well done Tom you've got the hot swim," shouted Rambo in a voice that was laced with just a hint of sarcasm.

Tom's face clouded momentarily as he saw a hidden thrust to Rambo's comments. He threw the ping-pong ball with the magic number 4 on it straight to Rambo who caught it.

"Not so hot is it?" Asked Tom defiantly.

Rambo lowered his head slightly into the chest of his camouflage jacket that he wore everywhere, probably including his bed, and shook his head. For a second I struggled to grasp the implications of this odd piece of happenstance and then it clicked. Rambo had thought that the draw was rigged, he had actually accused, admittedly subtly (a real culture shock that must have been, and a first for him) that Mike had taken a ball that had been heated up prior to the draw so as to give Ya Man the best swim. As all this sunk in the allocations continued. Mike himself got the Oak, another so-so opening day swim, and then Harry was given the Big Pads. Two of the big three had the best swims. I glanced across at Rambo who returned my gaze with raised eyebrows.

The last two swims the Deep Corner and the Pines went to the Laurel and Hardy of the carp fishing world Dave and Tony. They were the last two to join the syndicate. They were young, keen and inexperienced with only a few years fishing under their belts. They also only fished together, nobody had ever seen one of them on his own at a lake. They were the neo-duo. Shy, totally out of their depth in terms of carp fishing compared to even a third rater like myself, they were an easy butt of many a joke that went around our little club. I could well remember when I had been like them and at times when things were going hideously wrong I thought that maybe I still was. Consequently I gave them more time of day than many of the others and was therefore the closest thing the pair of them had to a friend within the syndicate. I knew that they had left the seat beside themselves for me. No one else would have sat there, no one had.

I smiled at the pair of them in turn. "Not a bad draw, boys. Not bad at all."

Tony took his left hand out between his legs. His hand was white, he shook it vigorously. "Bloody hand's gone to sleep," he explained sheepishly.

"So, gentlemen," said Tom, "that concludes the draw for the first round of the '93 S.S syndicate platter and here is the trophy that you will all be competing for." To mute surpass Tom produced an expensive looking silver plate. "This is the trophy that will be given by myself to the member who catches the most verified twenty pound carp this season." Murmur, murmur. This had taken us completely aback. Tom continued, "nobody else has been party to this, it is something that I have taken upon myself alone. If the rest of you are gracious enough to support me I hope it can become an annual event and the winners name will be inscribed on the cup yearly."

He passed the trophy around. I gazed at it. The Tom Watt Twenty Trophy was the legend engraved on the side. "Rolls off the tongue nicely," I said to Tony.

"Umm. Especially if Tom Watt takes the Tom Watt Twenty Trophy two times."

"Terrific."
"Tantalising."
"Tremendous," said Dave.
"I take it that you'll be competing as well, Tom." I asked full knowing the answer.
"Of course," smiled Tom.
"Better put his bloody name on it now," said Tradders. The rest of us laughed. Tom smiled benignly and as I looked at his handsome rugged face beaming away under an onslaught of sycophantic praise it suddenly dawned on me that I didn't like him. All this time it had been staring me in the face, here was a conceited, small time megalomaniac and I hadn't even realised it. Until now.

Now you may think it was jealousy that drove me to this conclusion. I can assure you that it wasn't, well only 50% of it was jealousy, he just suddenly irritated me. His mannerisms were all so clear to me now as if a fog had lifted from my perception, the false humility, the subtle put downs and scoffing all done so inoffensively and, the galling part, all backed up by the unarguable ultimate royal flush hand. The bastard was better at carp fishing than the rest of us.

After a few questions about the trophy and other minor items the meeting broke up. We would reassemble on the 15th of June on the lake and not before. We had a strict rule of prebaiting in the close season. You couldn't. Tom was adamant on it as were Harry and Mike. The rule had never been changed although some of the members had half-heartedly tried from time to time.

As we straggled out of the room I noticed Dave start to talk to Tom and Kipper while picking up the draw ping-pong balls with casual disinterest and distraction. I carried on down the stairs and straight out of the pub and started to wander down the road towards my car. Just as I got to it Rambo appeared alongside me, he was slightly out of breath. He had run to catch me before I left. My mind tumbled as to why he had made this effort to talk to me. We had hardly done more than pass the time of day for the six years we had known each other. I must admit I had always found Rambo an odd ball, what with his military clothing, jack boots and tattoos. Maybe if I'm honest I found him a bit frightening, he was after all, about 15 stone arranged in a 6'4" muscular inverted pyramid. The boy had shoulders.

"Here, Williams."
"Yes," I said awkwardly. This wasn't going to be easy for both of us.
"Look . . . umm. Look. You've got the Bay West right?"
"Right," I said and nodded slowly.
"And I've got the Bay East."
"Yeaahhsss." I said even slower, realising immediately that I was sounding like some kind of moron.
"Well. . . . Look. How would you like to come in on bait with me?"

I don't know whether I actually physically reeled or not but I certainly did mentally. Rambo. The Rambo, well not THE Rambo, but Rambo, the loner, asking someone else and even more incredulously that someone else being me to come in on bait with him? To be frank I'd have been less shocked if he'd have asked to bugger me in the back of my car there and then.

"Well... I....." I answered masterfully.

"Come on. What have you got to lose? I'm a better angler than you. More experienced."

He was right. "Yeah. Fair comment, but why? With me? What will you get out of it?"

"Look Williams. We're going to be fishing the Bay together. They might be in there or they might not. One bait in the same general area must be better than two. If they get on it we might slaughter them and....." He looked away. I wondered what the hell was coming next, absurdly my brain decided to addle and think irrationally. Maybe he was going to declare his undying love for me.

"And besides you don't seem a bad sort of bloke. Someone I could trust. Someone who could keep a secret." He turned and focused me straight in the eye. Jesus this was it. "I want me and you..." Bloody hell, "to prebait."

Relief! My mind cleared and with it my homophobia. I puffed out my cheeks, "Ummm, what...."

"Come on Williams let's go for it. Live on the edge for once in your life. Think of the look on that smug fucker's face if we catch more than him," said Rambo getting more and more animated.

"What, Watt?"

"Of course, Watt. Ya Man." He sneered with venom. It was this image that sold me the deal. God that would be great.

I made the snap decision that would spell serious trouble. "Too right, mate. You're on."

"Good." He slapped me on the shoulder. I managed to stay standing. "I'll be in touch." With that he disappeared off down the road.

I unlocked my car and got in, before I could start to crank the motor over Dave and Tony's faces appeared in the window. I wound it down. "All right, lads?" I asked cheerily in a facade at attempted normality.

"Not really," answered Dave.

"What's up then?"

"We've got something to tell you." Not another revelation. What was it this time? The pair of them were aliens from the planet Cypry. Dave continued. "You know the table tennis balls they used in the draw."

"Not personally, but yeah," I replied.

"There were two types of balls used."

"So? A ping-pong ball is a ping-pong ball is a ping-pong ball. Isn't it?"

"No," said Dave.

"Dave used to play table tennis for his county," said Tony butting in.

"Get to the point lads," I said a bit wearily.

"Well, the point is that the two balls that were different were the two balls for the

Island and the Big Pads." Dave paused for effect and I nodded as the smell of rat wafted up my nose. "You see table tennis balls come in three different grades, one star, two star and three star. Three star are the best quality and are used in pukka competitions, they are heavier and more solid because the walls are thicker. A table tennis ball is just cellophane type material with air in it. You can also buy unmarked balls from places like Woolies, you know just for kids, those things are paper thin. In the draw there were two Rizla balls and eight three stars. Anyone, especially Mike could easily tell the two good swim balls just by squeezing them with his thumb. They would press in much easier."

"So the draw was rigged," I said with brilliant insight.

"The draw was rigged. Harry and Tom won, with Mike's help."

"You're absolutely sure about this?" I asked, hoping that they were. Some deep perversity wanted me to believe that the big three were just plain cheats.

Dave confirmed. "Dead positive. It's too much to be a coincidence. The thing is what do we do about it?"

"You could always go and slash Tom's tyres for a start. I expect it'll make you feel better. Look I've got to go, don't tell anyone else. I'll be in touch. Ok?" I said echoing the parting phrase that had been Rambo's.

The pair nodded. This was all getting a bit heavy. I drove off home with a head full of thoughts that baffled and bemused me and which continued to baffle and bemuse me as I lay in bed. Sleep did not come easy that night. The cosy syndicate was sprouting a few warts. Little did I know that evening that this was just the beginning. For the S.S, to paraphrase Sir Winston, it was the beginning of the end.

Chapter 2

For the next few days I was constantly on edge. My girlfriend, Sophie, sensed this, no doubt using that deep intuition that women hold so dear.

"You're seeing somebody else aren't you?" She asked casually one evening while the pair of us were slouched on the settee, watching our favourite sitcom, Frasier.

"What?" I said with detachment, barely registering the question.

"I said, 'Are you seeing someone else?'"

"What in the sense of....?"

"Seeing somebody else! Yes, in that sense. You know, another woman?" Sophie said in a mixture of aggression and frustration.

"What on earth makes you come out with that kind of statement for Christ's sake?" I said with indignation.

"You've been a nervous wreck lately, that's why. Every time the phone rings you jump a mile. You must be hiding something," she reasoned, if that's the right word for it.

"So that means I'm seeing somebody else does it? Well, brilliant work Miss Holmes. What a clear, lucid mind you have. How uncanny of you to add two and two together and come up with forty seven million four hundred and eleven. Your logic would inspire Mr Spock. Why don't you go upstairs and go through my pockets and underwear to substantiate with physical evidence this amazing hunch of yours?" I blustered, and quite cleverly I thought, concealing the fact that I hadn't reckoned on being this transparent. The thought of Rambo phoning me up to give me the final details on our prebaiting campaign, of which I was now having serious second thoughts about, certainly had made me very nervous.

"I already have," admitted Sophie somewhat sheepishly.

"Jesus Christ. Did you check my dentures for pubic hairs that weren't yours?"

"You haven't got any dentures."

"No! But you might bloody need some in a minute!" Silence gripped the room. The proverbial pin went undropped. I watched in fascination as the colour drained from her face and her jaw fell like a heavy PTFE monkey climber on a back drop. Tears soon followed. I put my arm around her shoulder, my anger completely drained, and apologised.

"Come on. I'm sorry, I'm really sorry. You know I didn't mean it. Wipe away those tears now. Come on. It was a joke more than anything. Honestly."

Sophie gave me a wan smile. The phone rang. I picked it up.

"Williams?" The voice on the end asked abruptly.

"Yes?"

"Rambo here." It was my turn for the slack line and jaw treatment. The one time it happened to be the person I was dreading was the one time that I was off guard. I flicked my eyes towards Sophie in what could easily be construed as a furtive manner.

"Uhm, could you phone back later, it's a bit inconvenient now." This time Sophie's eyes narrowed and her brow furrowed. She mouthed the words 'Who is it?' as she nodded at the phone.

"No I can't phone back later," said Rambo, "look I've got all the bait, come round Thursday and you can help me roll it."

"How much have you got?"

"50 kilos."

"50 kilos!" I said somewhat hysterically. I glanced across at Sophie to see her eyes pop out on two metal springs hit the floor and recoil back into her sockets.

"We'll never shift that lot." I said desperately.

"Course we'll shift it. What the hell's a matter with you Williams. Just get your butt around to me by seven on Thursday."

"Where do you live?"

"Flat 2, 21 Plenham Place."

"Plenham Place, 21 flat 2," I repeated like a zonked out zombie.

"That's the one. See you at seven. Bring any bait making gear you've got, ok?"

"Er..yeah ....fine."

I put the phone down. Sophie was agog. I had gone from being possibly unfaithful to plausible drug runner via potential violent domestic.

"Who was that? What was all that about.......?" She started, but before she could ask the other 50 or so questions that were swimming in her head, I collapsed on the settee and told her the truth. I also told her not to tell another soul as if this got out, me and Rambo would be carp fishing history.

It was good to tell her, it got it off my chest and calmed me down. As we talked she and I got deeper into the clandestine nature of what Rambo and I were going to get up to. Sophie wasn't that interested in fishing, she had come with me on odd days, not to the syndicate water but elsewhere when the weather was nice and she could sunbathe, but this daring stunt seem to get under her skin and give her an adrenaline rush. She asked questions about when we were going to do the prebaiting, which was obviously at night, what sort of a headcase Rambo was and so on.

"It sounds really exciting all this sneaking about."

I laughed. "It won't be if we get caught."

"Whose going to catch you? There'll be no-one else there. As long as you can get to the water safely you'll be fine. I mean there's no buildings nearby are there?"

This was true. The only difficult bit as far as I could see was going to be where to leave the car. Sophie solved this with a generous offer.

"Why don't you let me take you to the water? I could be your driver. I could drop you and Rambo off as near to the lake as the road would allow, then I could drive off and come and pick you up later on. You can tell me roughly how long you will be and I can come and whisk you off after you've done the baiting."

This sounded fine to me and I told her that I would suggest it to Rambo and as long as he was happy she could be the official getaway driver.

Now that Sophie was in the know, things became easier at home and although I was still apprehensive I felt a lot more at ease with the whole situation. The thing that I was getting most worried about was how I would get on with Rambo. We were hardly bosom buddies, in fact it was doubtful if Rambo had a bosom buddy. He seemed an out and out loner, whereas myself, Mr Popular, could boast at least one bosom buddy at a stretch two, but he owed me money and could safely be discounted.

On Thursday, just after seven I stood outside the big old Victorian building that bore the legend 21, my finger hovering on the flat two bell button. I was about to find out how we would get on. I rang. In a few seconds Rambo appeared.

"All right, then?" He volunteered. His physical bulk towered above me even more than usual as he stood in the doorway with the added benefit of the threshold. It now crossed my mind that Rambo wasn't ever out to bugger me, that was patently ridiculous, he was going to cut me up into about twelve different pieces and slip me into a bath of lime.

"Yeah fine thanks," I lied.

Rambo looked covertly up and down the street. "Come in. Quickly."

The pair of us climbed the one flight of stairs to his flat door and in we went. The sight that greeted me was disconcerting. The walls were lined with paramilitary paraphernalia. Posters of every piece of military hardware you could think of and lots you couldn't were blue tacked all over the place. The floor and furniture were strewn with army boots, combat jackets and trousers, kit bags, berets and balaclavas. It looked as if a bunch of squaddies had stripped off, flung all their kit on the floor and left. Maybe they had.

"Is this all your gear then, Rambo?" I asked.

"Yeah. Sorry about all the mess but I just can't be fussed to clear up as I go. I normally wait until I have to do it."

In my opinion this was about a week ago but I let my considerations ride.

I followed Rambo into the kitchen where bags and bags of bait ingredients and dozens of eggs were stored on the worktop. The pile was at least three feet high. I walked over to the twenty or so bottles of flavour and picked one up. I looked at the additives, sweeteners, enhancers, aminos, essential oils, bulk oils, vitamins, minerals and realised that I was down for half of this. My terraced house was 100% mortgaged and without doubt I was into negative equity. All I could hope for would be a kindly bank manager and a personal loan. I could just see them lending me several hundred quid on a valuable, appreciating asset like carp bait.

"Jesus, Rambo. How much did this lot cost?" I asked fingering some of the more expensive merchandise.

"Don't you worry about the cost, Williams. I asked you to come in with me so the bait is my concern. You've just got to help me roll it and bait with it."

I let out a puff of air. "Well if your sure you don't mind?" I prayed he wouldn't change his mind.

"No. Right have you got any rolling gear with you?"

"Yep." I put my sports bag down and pulled out three mastic guns with their tubes, a sidewinder boilie maker and a couple of table type rollers for smaller sizes. "This is it, my entire bait kit."

Rambo nodded approvingly and smiled. Maybe I wasn't going to die after all. Perhaps not this evening at any rate.

"OK, mate. We've got a lot of graft to get through tonight so the quicker we get started the better. Look, I'll knock up the mixes and you can use your sidewinder and guns to whack out the boilies, then well put about 200 or so into boil in that." He gestured towards a huge metal container that looked like an old fashioned baby's bath. It was on the gas cooker and it successfully straddled all four burners, it would be ideal for mass boiling, it was big enough to boil two or three heads in. I smiled weakly.

"Where's your bowl for knocking up?"

Rambo snorted down his nose derisively and flicked his eyes at the mountain of bait. "Fuck the bowls, I'll use the sink."

True to his words apart from having sex with any containers Rambo started cracking eggs into the sink, adding all the flavours and whatnots with great care and then winding the mix in. I was impressed, pretty soon he was up to his elbows in what would turn out to be the most effective bait that I would ever fish with. (Now I know that all you punters out there would like to be told what the bait was. I know that recipe backwards, you don't get to mix up 50 kilos of bait and then just forget it, but it is information that I will not part with. Eventually I may be able to use it again and perhaps it will still be a winner, for all I, or the police, know Rambo might be using it this very moment in some foreign clime. So there we have it, or not in your case dear reader.)

I decided not to mention what Dave and Tony had told me and also decided not to ask Rambo about the inclusion of Sophie as confidant and getaway driver, these matters would best be left until later. As the pair of us mixed the night away, things got more and more intense. We worked in studious silence apart from the odd order that I received but never reciprocated. Spurred on by infectious enthusiasm the pair of us worked like Trojans, maybe Rambo always mixed bait like this, but I never had. I guess that most of us blokes would be grossly messy when we make bait but are kept vaguely in check by firstly our parents and then by our better halves' threats and cajoling. Without these controlling influences the cack tends to accumulate.

In Rambo's haste to keep me supplied with the mix and my own grim determination to try and run out of it, the pair of us worked ourselves up into brutal competition not only against the pile of bait that seemed reluctant to get any lower or narrower but with each other. In the frenzy of our contest and desire not to be out done things became increasingly manic. Niceties such as order and not making a mess were not so much thrown out the window as fired into orbit. Substantial lumps of the mix looked to have had the same idea as I flicked bits from my fingers, from the gun nozzles, and the rollers. Other more gravity obeying lumps lay littered on the floor where Rambo had transferred football sized lumps from the sink to my tray on the other side of the kitchen. Naturally he walked on them on his way back to the sink just to spread it all around a bit more. The kitchen looked as if a bomb had hit it, a bomb filled with red boilie paste, (that's the only clue you get!) that had splattered the six sides of our kitchen cube.

After two hours or so we were well into boiling. The large tin bath bubbled away like a witches' cauldron and so vivid was that image that I had to restrain myself from cackling when I dumped another hundred or so boilies into the seething tub and stirred them around for their allotted time. The tub had to be topped up with hot water from the tap every so often to stop it boiling dry. Rambo had thoughtfully cranked up his immersion heater stat to maximum so that we could keep the tub boiling much more easily. The missing water was obviously turning to steam, in fact with all the water vapour and heat from the four burners the kitchen felt like a sauna. My face felt as red as the mix. Beads of sweat ran down my forehead and into my eyes making them sting. The only relief was when I took the finished boilies into the other room to lay them out to dry. The relative coolness of that room was not to be savoured and I darted back into the kitchen intent on standing the heat. I imagined that the only things moving quicker than me and Rambo were his gas and electric meter dials.

By midnight I had cramp in my hands from squeezing the mastic guns and my right arm knew what it felt like to be a professional organ grinder as I constantly churned out a silent tune on the sidewinder. For some God forsaken reason we were making 16mm and 10mm boilies, 16mm with the sidewinder and 10mm with the guns and small rolling tables. Rambo said that he always felt happier with two sizes of bait at his disposal and who was I to argue, seeing as he had bought the bloody lot.

One o'clock had come and gone. It was now physically impossible to move an inch without treading on either boilie paste, boilies, egg shells, mix bags and empty flavour/enhancer/etc bottles. As well as this, a red mist hung in the air from the cumulative effect of heavy handed mix bag opening and had drifted down to form a red slurry that had converted the kitchen lino into a Martian landscape. A Martian landscape with trainer prints all over it.

The smell of flavour hung heavy in the air. When I went to the toilet for a leak I saw that I was dusted in powder mix, it also looked as if I had been snorting it. My nostrils were deep red. My hands were coated in the stuff and my penis now had a couple of John Dory finger prints on the top and bottom. I also noticed that Rambo had had the bath taken out, replaced it with a shower tray and put two upright freezers, one on top of the other in the extra space for boilie storage. Coming back into the sitting room there was a trail of red footprints from the kitchen that weaved in and out of Rambo's discarded garments onto the massive pile of drying boilies.

I licked my lips which tasted of something now very familiar, I was starting to wilt. I looked at my watch. Just gone two. I was knackered. I wearily shoved open the kitchen door and a plume of red steam wafted into my face. I squinted into the redness.

"Last mix, mate," called Rambo, triumphantly, gesturing towards a basketball sized dollop on my tray, "get that rolled and boiled and I'll start bagging up the boilies and putting them in the freezer."

Dutifully I knuckled under for one last push while Rambo used a dustpan to scoop the boilies into old Tesco bags that he had kept from his shopping trips. By three o'clock we were finished. All the ten or so thousand boilies were bagged and safely tucked up in the two freezers.

We were ecstatic, at least we were until we came back from the bathroom... shower room, to see the side effects of our intense efforts.

"God, what a mess," I said, "it'll take hours to clean up. I've got to be at work for eight and I'm shagged already."

"Forget it. I'll clean it all up after I've had some kip. I don't work at the moment so I've got time to do it," said a magnanimous Rambo. I wished he'd have been even more magnanimous and mixed all the bait himself during his never-ending weekends. I didn't want much did I? Tiredness does strange things to the mind.

"Nice one, Rambo. I tell you I'm absolutely shot," I slapped his upper arm, "I've got to go before I keel over. I'll tell you what I'll pop by tomorrow straight from work to pick up my bait gear and we'll have a little chat. We've been so engrossed by this tonight we've hardly said a word to each other. About half five all right?"

"Yeah. That's fine. We'll sort out a few tactics, rigs, baiting plan and all that." He gave me a smile. "You did all right tonight, Williams. I thought you might wimp out on me, but you didn't. I'll see you tomorrow."

Praise indeed! I didn't know whether to be chuffed or miffed. I plumped for chuffed and dragged myself off home.

It took me a good half hour in the shower to remove excess bait from my body. I had a mini-boilie's worth in my left ear that had made me think I'd gone slightly deaf and somehow a golf ball sized lump had found its way into my underpants. After showering I still smelt of..(ha-ha you won't see me slip up) ...flavour, but I was past caring. As soon as I hit the pillow I was gone.

Whereas years ago as a kid I would dream of the float that had burnt its likeness onto my retina after a long days float-fishing, that night I dreamt of boilies. Millions of them, swarming around me like a host of angry wasps. Wherever I fled they tailed me. However I fled, whether by car or bike, by plane or by foot they kept up with me. Wildly my arms flailed in desperation to keep them from me. I screamed and screamed in silence. Cricket bats, baseball bats, tennis rackets, fence posts, corner flags, all manner of implements passed through my hands as I vainly tried to swat the boilies back away from me. Each strength sapping, wild swing was useless, the boilies simply parted like the Red Sea did for Moses and my blows went straight through them. They buzzed and dived around my ears, I could even smell them. When I was totally drained by my useless efforts to thwart them I stood alone, exhausted. The boilies sensing I was there for the taking hauled themselves up into a massive, grotesque fist. It swept upwards as if on the end of some all powerful, invisible arm and thundered down towards my soon to be detached head. On impact I awoke with a start, my cheek stinging.

"Come on, Stinky, time to get up and earn a dollar. Boy were you dead to the world. I had to give you a slap to wake you up."

I blearily grinned at Sophie. My body was racked with niggling aches. The sidewinder had discovered muscles I never knew I had.

Friday on the building site dragged. Everyone who came near me wrinkled their nose and gave me a strange look. If any syndicate members had happened to bump into me our bait secret would have been out for sure. I told my fellow workers it was my new cologne. No one asked where I had got it.

After work I called in on Rambo. The flat was immaculate. All the mess was gone and Rambo had clearly decided to go the whole hog and clear up his military odds and sods. He made me a cuppa and we chatted. He had actually been in the army but had been discharged about four years ago. He never told me why and I didn't ask but this did explain why he hadn't fished a great deal in the early days of the syndicate but had certainly made up for it since being unemployed. I asked him how he could afford all his new gear that he had bought last season and the bait come to that. He tapped his nose and winked.

We chatted about the other members of the syndicate. Rambo had little time for any of them. I was intrigued to find out why he had asked me to come in with him but somehow the time never seemed right to ask. Besides there were two other things that headed my priority list. Eventually after talking a little about our respective fishing tactics I confided in him the knowledge that Dave and Tony had given me about the draw being rigged. Rambo went berserk.

"The fucking, cheating bastards," he said jabbing an index finger down at the floor. "I knew there was something funny going on, I just hadn't sussed how. I was barking up the wrong tree. I'll tell you this now Williams," he continued, eyeing me earnestly, " there is no way, and I mean no fucking way, that any of those three gits are going to win that trophy. I'd like to smack the lot of them."

One at a time or all together my money would have been on Rambo.

Discreetly I avoided reminding him of the fact that we were soon about to embark on some cheating ourselves but I couldn't avoid my next line that I had rehearsed in my head over and over. I waited until he had calmed down.

"There's one thing I want to ask you about the night we do the baiting."

"What's that?"

"Well, how would you feel if I asked somebody, you know outside the syndicate, to drop us off at some place close to the lake, we do the business and they pick us up? It'd save a lot of hassle and be safer."

Rambo considered this with a frown. "Yeah. But who?"

"My Sophie. She'd help. I've only got to ask her." I said, hoping Rambo wasn't psychic or had access to a lie detector. I didn't dare tell him I'd told her already, not without his ok.

He raised his eyebrows. "She'd do that would she? In the middle of the night and clear off and come back for us?"

"Sure."

"Yeah. Sounds good. Yeah. We'll get into night manoeuvre kit here, back pack of boilies, say 20 kilos each, she drops us off, we yomp to the lake, bait up, rendezvous with her and the car and pow! We're out of there and home and dry."

"Great," I breezed, "I'll sort it out with her tonight when I get home..... So, we'll just do the one bait blitz, then?"

"I think so. We'll do it 4 days before the 15th. That should give the carp long enough to find it and it'll be close enough for us to fish on the back of it. I think a more prolonged campaign might be better but it's too risky. No, we'll go with that."

"Fine. So, if I come here at say....?"

"Ten o'clock on the 11th of June. I'll have all the kit ready and your girl..." he looked at me.

"Sophie."

"Sophie can pick us up at midnight. Twenty minutes to the water at night by car. Ten to fifteen minutes to get to the lake. Another 30 to get the bait out, fifteen to get back, she can pick us up within the hour. Perfect."

"Sounds good to me." It did. Rambo's ex-army knowledge should make this little outing a tea-party. If by chance anything odd did happen I was happy to let his other outstanding ability come to our rescue. I was willing to wager that Rambo could duff up anybody we were likely to encounter. On his own, which was kind of important. What I would have lost money on was who that anybody was, although with the hindsight I promised not to use it should have been manifest.

Chapter 3

Date line; June 11th. Mission:- Prebait syndicate lake. No witnesses. Personnel:- Sophie Williams - drop off and pick up driver. Matt Williams - boilie lugger and catapult man. Rambo - camouflage expert, equipment provider, brains, brawn, leader, day and night team co-ordinator, financial sponsor and all round hard case. How well I remember that evening.

I left home at 9.30 for the twenty minute or so walk to Rambo's flat. I had left Sophie in a state of adrenaline and endorphin stupor. The girl was hyped. What is it with women that can allow them to have massive initial reservations about something and then they completely flip to being more keen than you are. I mean working at the CSA must have its high spots, its own rushes, it must prepare you for this sort of thing..but then again, maybe not.

I sauntered along with a casual gait that masked my own booming heart and I thrust my hands deep into my jean pockets. Their slight shaking could remain unnoticed unless I lost complete control and I would then cut the ridiculous figure of an outwardly calm man trying to remove a ferret from the gusset of his underpants through his pockets. I smiled to myself as this idea kicked around my head. An old women gave me a look she probably only used when staring at particularly gormless children. I winked at her with attempted rakish charm. She jerked her head away with a loud tut. I grinned even more wildly. This was it, this was living at the edge. Anarchy! Conforming was for others, tonight was the night where I set the parameters, where I made the rules or broke them. Well if Rambo said so I would, I thought with sudden a sobering of mind.

I rang the bell of flat 2, no. 21 Plenham Place. Rambo opened the door . It was five to ten. In the slightly fading light Rambo looked uncannily large and muscular. I thought to myself that I wouldn't like to meet him on a dark night and then realised that was exactly what I was going to do. Thank Christ we were on the same side.

"Hello, Williams. All right? Everything ok?"

"Yep, fine. Sophie's ready for the call. I left her pushing her fingers into a pair of her Mum's black driving gloves. She reckons that we ought to have hired a Jag. Being a getaway driver in a 1.1 Fiesta lacks a certain style."

Rambo laughed. "Come on let's go and get kitted up." I followed him upstairs into his flat and once again gazed at all the military posters that covered the lounge.

"In here," said Rambo as he entered his bedroom. Again I followed, again more posters, only this time it was a cornucopia of soft pornography. Centrefold images were splashed around the room with the same intensity as the Sunday Sport, i.e. everywhere you looked. Feminism and political correctness had failed to penetrate this male stronghold that was certain. I wondered who exactly had been penetrated in this intimidating room. What type of girl would find the ambience conducive to a bit of hanky-panky, or was Rambo a sad actor in a movie filmed in wankerama?

"Try a pair out of that lot, the socks are inside them."

Rambo had opened a large double wardrobe to reveal 20 or so pairs of army boots. Here was a man who could definitely claim to be the Amelda Marcus of the combat boot world. I chose one pair that looked to be one of Frankenstein's monster's cast-offs and slipped off my own trainers and tried them on. It was like putting my feet into the boxes my own shoes normally came in.

"A bit big," I understated.

Rambo rummaged amongst the other pairs and picked out the pair he obviously thought were the smallest. "Try these. Put the socks on over the top of your own, that'll help fill them out."

I did as instructed and did the strange shoe shop walk that we all do when we try out new shoes. With great exaggeration I walked up and down the small bedroom, bending my knees and pressing hard on the balls of my feet as I attempted to bend the soles of the boots.

"Yeah not bad. I won't have to worry about being blown away by the wind that's for sure," I said giving Rambo a grin.

He nodded and fished out a pair of camouflaged trousers and jacket from the wardrobe shelf. "Get these on while I start to load the backpacks."

Rambo left me to get ready. The trousers and jacket fitted quite well. Both items had that worn in feel of comfort, any stiffness or newness had been washed and worn out ages ago. I put the boots back on and looked at myself in the mirror that had been fitted to one of the wardrobe doors. I looked all right, almost passing for the real thing. The uniform makes the man so they say. I ran my fingers over the jacket breast pocket in idle distraction and felt a tiny rip that I hadn't noticed in the mirror. It turned out not to be a rip but a hole. Queasily I bent my arm behind my back, just below my shoulder blade and groped my thumb around. Sure enough I found another hole that lined up with the one in the front. If the uniform made the man I would have had a bullet straight through the chest and out the other side. Surely not. I went to find Rambo to ask him. Why did he have different sized shoes and clothes was another teaser that had concerned me?

He was in the kitchen shoe horning another bag of boilies into a backpack, a camouflaged backpack.

"Here Rambo? These holes in this jacket are they?"

"Bullet holes?" He said nonchalantly, "yeah. One of my team bought it in that very jacket you're wearing."

"When?" I screeched, scarcely believing what I was hearing.

"About two years ago."

"Who the bloody hell were you fighting two years ago? I thought you'd been discharged four years ago?"

"I was. Two years ago I was doing a bit of moonlighting..... in Africa. Angola to be precise."

My mind grappled with what Rambo had said. "You were a mercenary?" I said shocked.

"Well we've all got to pay for those new carbon rods and baitrunners somehow. It is my trade after all."

"Jesus! I don't know whether I can wear this thing now I know that...."

Rambo cut me dead. "Just think yourself lucky I managed to get all the blood out," but he smiled afterwards and I got a grip of myself. At least it explained his relative affluence and all the kit he had to clothe his dirty dozen or however many there were. Any thought as to how he got the jacket back off of the guy who 'bought it' went on the back burner. Some things are better not to know. I wondered if there was an expression, 'dead man's camouflage jacket' and decided there better not be.

By just after eleven we were ready. I cut a mean figure in full combat kit. Boots that could stove your head in with a mere flick of the ankle, camouflaged trousers, jacket, beret and backpack. I had a face that Al Johnson would have been proud of, (blacked out with greasepaint, for non fans) and to top it all I was armed with an Uzi 9mm catapult. Actually it was an Uzi 10 and 16mm catapult because that was the bore of the stinky bullets I possessed. Guessing by the weight of my backpack I had about 6,000 rounds. Rambo, now also in full attire, had the same ammunition only he would use the throwing stick bazooka. Weapons technology is a wonderful thing.

I phoned Sophie. It rang twice and she answered. "Hello, 456342."

"This is Sidekick. Operation Baitrun is go." I whacked the phone down. I was playing it up, the excitement was making me a bit heady. I must have looked a complete arsehole to someone like Rambo who had played war in real life and more pointedly in real death.

We gave Sophie ten minutes and then we took all our gear down into the common entrance front door hallway. Rambo cracked open the door to see the blue Fiesta and Sophie at the wheel.

"Ok, lets go," he said just like the American footballers used to on Channel 4.

The pair of us walked out onto the pavement and then to the car, I put the two backpacks into the boot while Rambo crammed his massive body into the back. Just as I was about to climb into the passenger's seat a policeman came around the corner and gave me an old fashioned look.

"T.A's. Night manoeuvres," I said jauntily. He gave me the thumbs up.

I flicked my right wrist forward and gave Sophie an anxious look that said 'move it". She put the Fiesta into first gear and promptly stalled it.

"Sorry," she said sheepishly and over-revved the car so much I thought the valves might pop out through the head. We screeched off, all three of us obeying Newton's third law of motion namely, every action has a re-action equal and opposite.

I turned to Rambo whose knees seemed to be up around his ears. "Not much legroom in the back is there?"

"Not really," he just managed to blurt before a too briskly taken corner sent him lurching across the back seat. He clawed himself back upright. "Do you think you could tell your good wife that we only need to get there alive. Speed is not essential. We are trying to pull off a very quiet unspectacular mission. So far we couldn't have been more bleedin' obvious if we'd announced ourselves with flares and a loud hailer."

I raised my eyebrows at Sophie although it was hardly likely that she could tell with a face as black as your hat. "Calm down, girl," I said. "You got a diving boot on your right foot?"

"It looks like you've got them on both feet," she said sarcastically, but she smiled as she said it and got back to her normal style of driving.

The journey took part in silence as all three of us became introverted with our own thoughts. I caught sight of Sophie checking out the large figure in her rear view mirror several times. She had never met Rambo although I had mentioned him many a time even before I had become embroiled in this latest escapade. Rambo remained taciturn and consequently answered none of the questions of mental stability that were undoubtedly ploughing across Sophie's brain. Rambo had always been a bit of an enigma amongst the syndicate members. A loner, uncommunicative and of course physically menacing. I guess we had always had him down as a thug, now I was less sure. Ok we hadn't exactly traded life stories and opinions but I was way past the stage of being frightened of the bloke, I could even say I was nearly at ease with him. More at ease with Rambo than the little night exercise we were about to embark on that was for sure.

In twenty minutes we were poodling along the leafy lane that had the syndicate's car park turn off. We drove straight past it, craning our necks for any sign of life. A futile gesture as anybody crass enough to be attempting what Rambo and I were obviously wouldn't use it. Like we weren't! Some 300 yards down the road we pulled over and Sophie turned off the engine and lights.

"Ok," said Rambo, "let's synchronise our watches. I've got 23:43. 43 minutes past eleven o'clock." Sophie and I struggled to set our watches by the cruddy interior light that must have been at least a five watt bulb. Good old Fords.

"23:44......now," said Rambo. We both confirmed. "Right then Sophie, you come back for me and Matt at one o'clock. Wait for ten minutes. If we don't show, just go."

"What and call the police?" Sophie asked somewhat confused.

Rambo snorted. "Definitely not. If there is any problem that has made us late we will deal with it. Got that?" Sophie nodded.

"Right, let's go," said Rambo for the second time that evening. Maybe it was a favourite phrase of his.

I got out and slid the passenger seat forward and Rambo uncoiled himself from the back. We took the backpacks out and put them on. I blew Sophie a kiss as she started up the car and drove off. I stood and waved to her.

"Come on Williams, you'll see her in a bloody hour. Were not going off to fight

World War III." He was right, we were off to start the syndicate's own World War I.

I followed Rambo off the road and over the wooden fence that bordered the land that our lake was on. It was a cloudy night and virtually pitch black. I was thankful for the pencil beam torches that we both had. I was never a keen night angler, I couldn't sleep through the hours of darkness and much preferred to catch during the day when everything seemed much easier and more enjoyable. However, tonight was a different matter. Darkness was a considerable ally rather than the usual hindrance, she cloaked us from prying eyes, she was a partner in our complicity.

Ruggedly I followed Rambo as he stealthily cut through the woodland. Despite his size and therefore his weight he was deceptively nimble and light-footed. He never trod on a fallen branch and always held back branches and undergrowth that would have either smacked me in the mouth or caused me to stumble. Like an automaton I shone my torch on the backs of his heels and trudged after him. If the world had suddenly become flat and he'd gone over the edge I would have gone lemming-like after him. My only thought process was to follow as quietly as I could.

After five minutes of walking my breathing had become heavier underlining my lack of fitness despite having a manual job. The air rasped in and out of my chest creating an imagined cacophony of noise. I tried holding my breathe to listen to Rambo's breathing, but his seemed as sedentary as a sleeping cats. When I started to breathe again I had to do it faster and deeper to re-supply my oxygen diminished body.

Rambo stopped and turned. "Fuck me boy, I'd like to have you on the parade ground for a few hours to sort you out," he said in hushed tones that thankfully lacked malice.

On we went. I had no idea of our whereabouts in relation to the lake until some ten minutes later when we arrived adjacent to the path that ran around the entire lake and forked back to the car park. The path was only two yards wide and as we came out of the woods and onto it there was one of the main features of our lake. The oak tree. Some five or so yards past the tree was the swim that bared the name The Oak. What a witty lot we were.

I could now fathom out the route that Rambo had taken me on. It was now a simple case of following the path north, stopping first at the Bay East and then around the bay feature itself to the Bay West swim.

We didn't move on the path straight away. Rambo held a finger up to his lips and we both listened. All seemed as it should be, a gentle breeze rustled the fully leafed trees but nothing else stirred. We still listened. We kept on listening, I wondered if Rambo had nodded off standing up, but no, he was just applying some field technique that said 'X' would make itself audible if you listened for 'Y' amount of time. Eventually he was satisfied and we moved. I had literally gone two paces when a moorhen blasted off one of those banshee screams for which they're famous. I went into orbit and upon re-entry gave Rambo a gesture of annoyance.

"Natural noise," he whispered, "we were listening for unnatural noise."

"Didn't sound very bloody natural to me. Bastard things. The times I've jumped when those things squawk, normally I think it's my Optonic going off......"

Rambo put his hand across my mouth. "Easy boy. Come on."

Off we went. Suddenly things became easier to see. The cloud cover had been wafted away by the breeze and half a moon and a thousand stars came out to watch us. I looked up to see, apart from a few straggling clouds a now clear sky. I wondered if they had carp fishing on other worlds as I gazed up at the thousands of stars twinkling above me. It was an awe inspiring sight like it always is, but that night it seemed special.

We arrived at the Bay East and Rambo took off his backpack and laid out a small ground sheet. On this he tipped his load of boilies.

"Right let's get them in the lake. Don't worry too much about where you put them. Put some in the margins and then spread'em far and wide."

It seemed fair enough. The bay had little in the way of features, no pads or weeds as such so it was virtually a margin/open water swim. I grabbed the first of many handfuls and chucked them in the margin to the left and Rambo put them to the right. I cringed as the first few hit the water. The noise seemed deafening. Maybe it was all in the mind because it was a covert operation but every plop seemed to reverberate around the lake. As the ripples spread across the moonlit sheen of the surface I was convinced we'd be heard miles away. When I started with the catapult it got worse. Now there were two noises, the elasticated thwack of the catty and the multiple plops of the boilies. I fired with demented speed and questionable accuracy although I was pretty sure that most of them went in the lake. I felt like I was in some bizarre game of which the sole intention was to dump 6,000 boilies into a large puddle as quickly as possible. Rambo and I must have looked like a couple of nodding donkeys on speed as we relentlessly bobbed up and down to grab bait, fire it out and then, dip, reload and out again. I could feel sweat running down my forehead but the torch revealed fewer and fewer boilies. In fifteen minutes we were done.

Rambo carefully checked for loose baits lying around. No evidence as well as no witnesses. We marched off to the Bay West swim and repeated the exercise with my backpack of boilies. By the time we had woken up the whole of Sussex, or so my paranoia suggested, it was 12:35. We had done well. We simply had to get back to the rendezvous in 25 minutes which was comfortable. We retraced our own steps around the bay past the Bay East swim and back to the Oak. Suddenly Rambo froze and lifted up his index finger to point upward towards the sky. Like a klutz I looked heaven bound.

"D'you hear that?" He whispered.

I listened intently. Nothing. "There!" Said Rambo triumphantly. "Voices. Definitely voices." This time I heard them.

"Come on let's go," I said.

"Ok, but carefully."

I turned to head back to the road via the way we had come earlier but found myself alone. I looked to see Rambo slinking off towards the voices, following the path around to the south of the lake. I ran after him and put my hand on his shoulder.

"What are you doing going that way. Let's get out of here for Christ's sake," I said in excitable whispers.

"Calm down, boy. We are going to see what the hell is going on and who the bloody hell is doing it. Follow me closely. Say nothing and don't use your torch." And with that on he went. I was powerless to do anything other than exactly what he said despite the fact that it went against every nerve and sinew in my body. The last thing I needed was confrontation with some axe wielding somnambulist.

Rambo moved quickly and stealthily around the path. The voices became clearer as we past the Little Pads swim. The odd word became intelligible as we got to the next swim round, the Wide swim. It was here that Rambo slipped back into the woodland. I nipped in after him, some five yards back from the path we both laid down on our stomachs. As I lay there it suddenly struck me that the other person or persons were either incredibly stupid or incredibly arrogant. They made no attempt to hide themselves with quietness but seemingly acted as if it were some Sunday afternoon jaunt they were on. Arrogant. The first idea of who we might be dealing with slipped into my mind.

In a couple of minutes two figures appeared. "Well old chap here's your first day swim, shall we stick some bait in?"

I knew those unctuous tones anywhere. It was Tom Ya Man Watt, carp fisherman by Royal Appointment and by definition of the first day draw the other cheating bastard, along with myself and Rambo, was Harry. Of course the pair of them were cheating bastards twice over because they had manipulated the first day draw to get the best swims. Rambo and I had only started cheating when firstly; he thought they were cheating and secondly; when Dave and Tony confirmed they were cheating to myself and then I confirmed it to Rambo.

Life can get bitter can't it? What do you do? Grin and bare it taking the moral high ground (myself on my own)? Or do you join them to try and beat them at their own nasty little game, still taking the moral high ground by saying they started it (myself with Rambo the Righteous Rocket up my backside)? Do two wrongs make a right? To be honest even by then it had got past all that, even by then it was personal. It was all about putting one over that smug bastard Watt and his two cronies Harry and Mike. The more we found out about Watt the more it became clear that he was the opposite to the image he projected. This outwardly kind, benevolent all wonderful syndicate leader was turning out to be a total shithead.

"Good idea," said Harry. "We'll put out a few hundred here and then go back and do yours."

The pair of them started putting out the bait before their unknown audience. They said little during the five minutes or so that we could hear them. I was praying for some vital revelation to be told but this was reality and not some T.V thriller where undoubtedly we would have had the beans spilt. Soon the pair of them were gone.

We stayed put until the plop plopping of them baiting up The Island had ceased. Rambo and I eased our way up from our prone positions.

"Bastards!" We said in unison and laughed.

"Come on Williams we have got to get a wriggle on if we're to meet your lady on time." He looked at his watch. "We've got 15 minutes left if she waits the full ten."

The pair of us got out onto the path and Rambo started to jog. It was an apparently effortless lope of great athleticism and fluidity. If I had reckoned on being unfit coming out to the lake I was a total wreck going back. My breathing was hard and fast while my lungs went into phlegm production overdrive. Soon my legs felt as if they had been turned to some base metal, namely lead. I knew this was because of lactic acid build up as I'd read it in a magazine but the knowledge didn't make it any better. It was only the fear of losing Rambo and getting hopelessly lost that overcome the fear of dying from exhaustion and managed to keep me going.

My torch shone a wild erratic beam that danced up and down on Rambo's back as I just managed to hang in with him. I had stitch, my boots hurt, the backpack straps dug into my shoulders, my lungs were on fire and my legs were beginning to disobey the orders I was giving them when thankfully, and not a moment too soon, we came to the fence . Rambo vaulted over, I crawled over. Mercifully Sophie was there waiting. We piled in and Rambo recounted the nights deeds to her as I gasped for life giving oxygen and sweated profusely.

We dropped Rambo off at his flat and then went home. I ditched the damp kit onto the floor and had a long hot shower. Totally spent, I wearily walked into our bedroom. Sophie was on top of the bed in her most provocative underwear.

"Come here, hunky. I want you to screw my brains out. All this excitement has made me as horny as hell."

"Well, you're on top then," I said with as much enthusiasm as is possible when you're totally knackered. I laid back and thought not of England, because they didn't have a match, but of carp and Watt and Rambo and cheating and then Watt again and him cheating again and how Rambo or myself just had to win that trophy. I never let her or myself down. I think my anger pulled me through.

Chapter 4

Rambo and I kept in touch by phone after the prebaiting night. Several conclusions were made about that evening but the two biggest mysteries couldn't be satisfactorily answered. One was why Mike hadn't been there to complete the triple alliance of big wigs and the second was the small amount of bait Tom and Harry had put out. Logic said that the pair of them were on a 'little and often' campaign which Rambo had preferred but had decided against for fear of detection. As to Mike, well maybe he had other fish to fry or simply was unavailable on the night that we were there. Rambo wasn't concerned about Mike, for all he cared he could have been enslaved by aliens from the planet Purgatory but the Tom\Harry baiting had him worried. It was how he had wanted to do it so by definition he thought that method to be superior. Rambo was sure that round one had been taken by the enemy. He consoled himself by hoping that our bait would be better.

As the gauntlet had by now been well and truly hurled to the ground both Rambo and myself were really up for the Tom Watt Twenty Trophy. Despite sounding as if it came from the most alliterate headline writer's pen it had got under our skins. Here was a tangible trophy to test our talent. (Sorry!). Tom Ya Man Watt had unwittingly given Rambo and I something solid that, providing one of us could win it, would shatter all that he stood for. If one of us could win, and believe me I had no personal ambitions other than Watt not winning, it would stuff the concept of his smug superiority right up his rear end. All the others in the syndicate wanted to win as well, that was for sure but only in a half-hearted manner. They were quite ready to concede to Watt's fishing ability, which despite everything was considerable. Also none of them, apart from Dave and Tony who had sussed the draw rigging, had any knowledge of the lengths Watt and his two other cronies would stoop to. Therefore they lacked the motivation to win at all costs because they had no access to Watts treachery and were not angered by it. In hindsight reader, I wasn't at the 'all costs' cross-roads yet. That was to come later. Nevertheless at that time we were merely matching the enemy virtually tit for tat, fighting fire with fire if you like. Perhaps our biggest card was that no-one else knew of my alliance with Rambo. We had decided to act as if we were, well, as normal. That meant Rambo the loner and me, Williams, the nondescript face in the crowd. However, back to my story.

June 15th soon came. All those tackle jobs had been done and for my part with a great deal more enthusiasm than usual. Reels cleaned and greased, new line loaded. Rods repaired. Rigs all ready. Rucksack completely cleared, now devoid of debris. Batteries bought for optimum Optonics and fine flash photography. Camera kitted out with Kodak. Accessories acquired. Scales, sling, sack, and stove sorted. Bivvy and bedchair and it was all there..... in the back of the van. Oh yeah and there was food and toilet paper and all that shit.

I had decided to take a weeks holiday to coincide with the first week of the season, Rambo would also fish the first week of the season as well. In this week with constant feeding we hoped to set right any shortcomings of our initial baiting campaign. A week was the maximum time that the first day draw allowed you to stay in one swim, (I know that sounds a bit paradoxical but we are only carp fishermen). If things were going well Rambo simply planned to stay on and move into my swim when I went back to work. In theory he could then fish that swim until he either died of boredom, exposure or chronic self abuse, or admittedly taking it to the extreme he ran out of time on midnight March 14th. Our most wild dreams never imagined us lasting for more than four days or so in the bay. Given the best luck in the world the fish would surely move out in that time, providing they were up there in the first place of course and you wouldn't have bet your house on that if previous form was any yardstick.

Rambo and I envisaged some sort of move in the week. Where we moved to, all depended on how many others stuck it out, how well they were doing and so on. In years past it often turned out to be a fishing version of musical chairs. I can remember one year when Kipper and Tencher had swapped swims both swearing blind that their swim was dead and that the other had definite fishy signs. How the rest of us laughed, how the rest of us took the piss.

There were ten swims and there were ten syndicate members. This was no coincidence. There was probably enough room to have doubled the amount of swims if you were prepared to turn round quickly and get the adjacent bloke's rod tip in your eye. An exaggeration but you get the drift. All of us had experienced over crowding on waters, people doing side flick casts and whipping a sandwich out of your mouth with a bent hook rig. Getting cast over, fishing the left hand margin and someone comes along and fishes their right hand margin, putting in so much bait that your 20 or so select offerings were buried under a mountain of tiger nuts and so on. It was this type of thing that you joined a syndicate to avoid, and the novelty of being able to fish with three rods instead of the bog standard club water two.

On our lake with ten swims you had room, you could stretch your legs out under the table, so to speak. You could do a bit of stalking within your swim as most boasted at least 40 to 50 yards of bank and you could spread your gear about and feel secluded. Alternatively you could pair up in a swim to chat and discuss important topics like the girls in the Sunday Sport when the action was less than forthcoming and yet not feel like a pair of sardines. It was nice, but at opening week with a full compliment you had no real chance to move onto fish. This had never unduly concerned me but now it did. The thought of Watt racing into an early lead while Rambo and I fished the swimming pool scenario out on a limb in the bay would be a situation that would be very difficult to cope with. The words 'powerless' and 'impotent' leapt to mind.

All this ran in and out of my mind as I drove on auto pilot to the lake. It was two in the afternoon, all the members were meeting about two-ish in the car park. From there we would all lug our ridiculous amounts of tackle and food and bait down to our allotted swims and make ready for midnight and the off.

I pulled into the narrow turning that lead to the car park. I was very nervous, this would be the first time that I would see Watt since the meeting in the 'Black Horse' and the first time I'd hear him since the prebaiting night. I also had to remember not to be too familiar with Rambo, and I don't mean in that sense either. I had to control my new friendship with Rambo and my new dislike of Watt. I was only going bloody fishing but it felt as if I was involved in some diplomatic convention or politics. I had to say what people expected me to say and not what I really thought. It was then as I parked the van that I realised I done this 90% of the time in any case and my worries slipped from me. This was no different than bullshitting the boss or white-lying the wife.

I got out the van, a brief look around suggested that everyone else was there.

"Late again then, Matt?" said Tradders with a big smile. He was all right, a nice guy.

"Go and check those split canes of yours for woodworm, you old duffer. And I hope you've put new batteries in those bits of silver paper you use for indicators," I countered playfully.

Tradders, real name John Smith of all things, was the traditionalist, hence the nickname. Chris Yates was a bit of a guru to him. Split cane rods, Mitchell 300's (not even Tradders was daft enough to use a centre pin), no buzzers, a tent instead of a bivvy, all old gear from the 60's that he was happy enough to use because he said it was good enough for him then and it was good enough now. He didn't need to cast to the horizon so didn't buy the tackle to do it. He was in his late 50's, his tackle from the 60's but he wasn't completely jammed in a bygone age. He still fished boilies and a hair rig but was less stereotyped than the average modern angler. On occasions when things were hard he would freeline and experiment with presentation and baits, often with an older method and a bait considered to be blown, whereas I would stay clipped up behind 3 ozs leads boilie bashing. When the fish were having it he would be back to my sort of method. He normally caught more than I did but despite this I had a lot of time for him.

"Now you're here I think Tom is going to have words about his trophy. A few rules and regulations," said Tradders shaking his head. "I can see all this coming to trouble you know." It was the most succinct observation he was ever likely to have.

"Why's that then? It's only a bit of fun," I said fibbing freely.

"We'll see. I'm just being a pessimist I suppose. It's the competitive aspect of it that worries me."

I looked up at his face but his eyes were elsewhere, he was looking at Tom who was beckoning us all with some impressive arm flapping.

"GENTLEMEN, PLEASE. IF YOU COULD BE SO KIND," he called, and like obedient dogs the nine of us formed a semi-circle around him.

"Welcome gentlemen to the start of another season. I am pleased to see you all and glad that you have all decided to start your respective campaigns off on our lovely little water. Good luck to you all, although as I suspect in time honoured fashion some shall have more fortune than others. Such is life." Homespun philosophy I thought, how cute. "Now as you know this year is the start of the Tom Watt Twenty Trophy being available to the ultimate winner. Now one amongst you has stressed a mild dislike for this. This has been voiced privately to me alone and not perhaps when it should have been at the last meeting when all concerned could listen. The lone voice amongst you has disagreed with the competitive element involved," I glanced across at Tradders knowing full well it must have been him. Tom continued, "now I know that the rest of you are enthusiastic about this and have no such hang ups. So let me stress for our one individual and to reiterate to the rest of you. THIS IS FOR FUN. This is about a friendly, enjoyable, light-hearted bit of pleasure that will hopefully give you all an extra interest and challenge for this season. We are friends bonded by a love of our sport. We are people of principle. Not one of you will stoop below those ideals and I know this to be a fact. Anyone who doubts you has less respect for you than I have, that is for certain. Besides some of you may get to be famous because of it." Tom paused, while I admittedly admired his cunning speech and wondered what the hell he was on about now.

"Yes gentlemen you will be pleased to know that I have been given a commission to write a series of articles about our lives this season. So look forward to checking your names out in the monthly editions of Carpworld, catch some good fish and you may have a photo of yourself in there as well."

He had done it again. Tom went on to say how no details of how to reach our water would be submitted, no photographs that showed obvious land marks etc and so on. He then said that all twenties need only be weighed-in by one other member and sacking was permissible if you happened to be fishing alone. He himself would come out and verify the fish when contacted, at any time he was at pains to point out.

Smiles were everywhere apart from Rambo and Tradders. The latter was gazing at the ground presumably looking for a suitable hole to crawl into. Rambo never smiled much so it was doubtful that anyone would realise that he was fuming with the hypocrisy of it all. Even Dave and Tony looked as happy as a couple of sand boys. I was sporting my best inane grin but I felt the veins in my temple throb and bulge like writhing worms under my skin. Given access to a machine gun Tom would have looked like a piece of Swiss cheese.

We dispersed and started to play at pack mules and sherpas. Donkey Dave barely visible underneath a mass of Kevin Nash holdalls and rucksacks came past me as I opened my van up and started asking me which was his best side should he be featured on the cover of Carpworld with a twenty in his arms and a trophy in front of him.

"I shouldn't waste too much time worrying about that possibility, you're more likely to be hit by a meteorite." I snapped. "But, if the rest of us all die and you manage to fluke one out and win by default, keep the weigh sling over your head," I said aggressively, "and keep your back to the camera."

"Only asking, misery guts," he whined sounding hurt and staggered off. I was seething too much to care about a fragile ego and threw my gear out of my van and onto the ground and slammed the doors shut.

"All right mate," said Tencher, "a bit heavy handed aren't we?"

"Oh, bad morning at work."

"Well don't start thinking about bloody work my son, this is the start of the season," said Tencher in the way that you might try and encourage a wimpy schoolboy.

"Ok Dad," I said with little good humour. Ok, with no good humour. He shrugged and left me alone. I climbed in the back of the van in an elaborate ploy to check that I had got everything. I sat and took in a few deep breaths. When you go through life being a fairly easy going type of bloke who suffers fools quite gladly and generally gives people the benefit of the doubt it comes as a shock to be really annoyed by them. Well not 'them' but one person who then gives you the downer for everyone, which is even worse. Here I was about to embark on my favourite week of the year doing the sport I love and I was pissed off something rotten. It was all Watts fault. If he wasn't such a loathsome, odious fraud coupled with a desire for acknowledgement and an ego the size of England I could have probably coped. But he was and I couldn't.

"How can he say what he just said and be doing what he's been doing?" I muttered to myself incredulously. "What a fucking two faced bastard. God, I'd .."

"You all right in there?" It was Rambo.

"Not really. I'm just about to go supernova."

"Save your aggression for the fishing," said Rambo like some wise old man. "By the time you've carted that pile of crap you call fishing tackle down to the Bay you'll be so goosed you couldn't explode enough to break out of a Christmas cracker."

I laughed and calmed down a bit. "Here, the others aren't watching you are they?"

"Pphh," said Rambo derisively. "They've all loaded up and lurched off, the sad gits. I mean it is after half two and fishing starts at midnight. It makes me chuckle, I mean what is it with people? They all know what swim they're going to fish, they've got more than nine hours to set up and get ready and the dorks are virtually racing each other down the path."

"That's adrenaline, mate. I guess it's what fishing can do to you. I've done it before."

Rambo gave me a look that said that he could well believe it. "Well I never have. Discipline you see. If I needed to be down there first I'd trample the lot of them flat but I don't need to be so I take my time and don't rush things through. One of them will be back up for something they've forgotten or couldn't carry. One trip at a steady pace is all that is required. So..... are you going to get out of that rust bucket or are you going to stay in there grouching to yourself like some demented van-hermit?"

"Didn't he used to play up front for Holland?" Rambo remained untouched by my levity. "Ok I'll get out," I said a little self consciously.

The pair of us loaded ourselves up. Now I thought that I was pretty well kitted out when it came to tackle but Rambo looked to have got enough gear for two people. He had a rucksack that looked big enough to put a small family car in, with bedchair attached and he had two rod holdalls that he slung across each shoulder on the diagonal, the way Mexican gunslingers favoured their bullet belts. He then tucked a caravan sized bottle of butane under one arm and gripped a huge carryall with the hand of that same arm, in the other arm he had a large 5 gallon water bottle. The weakling carried nothing in his teeth. Every item of kit including the butane bottle had got S.S stencilled on it in sharp, black pointy block capitals. If the Third Reich had ever sponsored fishing Rambo would have been up in court on a trademark copying rap.

We set off down the path, Rambo first. At first I was a bit concerned that we would look like a partnership as we came into view of the others but this relied on my stupid assumption that I would be able to keep up with him. Despite the fact that he was carrying at least twice maybe even three times as much weight as myself and his insistence that he was taking it easy, his bedchair was soon yards in front of me. It bounded along due to the fact that it was attached to the marquee sized rucksack which in turn was attached to Rambo. Who had marquee sized lungs by the look of it and may also have had a nuclear powered body. As I watched him stomp effortlessly out of view through sweat stung eyes, I wondered if he was some sort of android. A sort of Terminator that liked to do a bit of carp fishing, either that or he was on steroids. Surely no-one could be that strong naturally. Again I thanked my lucky stars to have such a useful ally, some-one who was blessed with the in-built ability to smash the living daylights out of virtually anyone or anything that you could care to mention. And a lot you couldn't.

Eventually I came to the divide in the path where it split both ways and formed a perimeter around the whole lake. This one and only 'T' junction was virtually by the swim called The Island where His Greatness, Tom Ya Man Watt was no doubt setting up for a productive session. West or left at the junction took you around past the Deep Corner (Dave), the Big Pads (Harry), The Pines (Tony), First Twenty (Tradders) and then my swim the Bay West. If I went counter clockwise or East or right I went past The Wide (Kipper), Little Pads (Tencher), The Oak (Mike), The Bay East (Rambo) and then around the bay to my swim. It was like a mini M25 orbital, one lane with passing or overtaking done with caution. I decided to go right so that I could see Rambo, the distance either way being so similar as to be of no real consequence.

The lake was visible from the path except for the many small pockets of dense foliage. The six or so yards from the path to the actual waters edge allowed a fair degree of privacy. Most people bivvied up close to a large bush or rhodie for a sense of snugness and isolation. You really had to walk to the waters edge to check to see if a swim was free or not because of this. There were also a fair few choices of bivvy positions in each swim although on the whole two or three were popular and used most of the time.

I trudged around and arrived at the Bay East, Rambo was propped up against a tree that bordered the path smoking a fag.

"Keep going around to your swim boy, I'll be round in a minute," he said in a conspiratorial voice and winked at me. 'Jawohl mein Commandant' I thought but not loud enough so that he could hear telepathically.

At last I got to the Bay West. Home for the next week. I was shagged. Rambo had been right again, my seething temper had petered out to a nagging gripe. I let my gear fall off my body and felt that gravity forgot me for a few minutes as I moved freely without the weight of tackle. The sensation was short lived and soon I was pulling 12 stone again and feeling every ounce of it. Slowly I started to unpack my rucksack taking out my overwrap first, then I pulled my umbrella out from my holdall and unceremoniously thrashed its pole into the hard ground with my rubber mallet. This was always my opening move in the game of chess I was about to embark on namely the long session.

I slowly, (this was due to the effects of the sherpa run from base van to base camp rather than any methodical action on my part) started to set up. Rambo soon bowled up and interrupted me. He had brought me a cup of tea and a two way radio. He told me how to use it and suggested only to do so when one of us had vital information such as fish movement, details of a catch or news of the others.

Out of view of those others behind a large run of rhodies we talked about Watt's little speech. Rambo was also of the opinion that Watt had used one of the inexhaustible, (we hoped not) supply of aces that the cunning sod may have up his sleeve or tucked down his waders or wherever. Being successful while fishing the circuit waters and rubbing shoulders with other elite 'names' had given him the opportunity to write many articles over the years for various magazines and papers. He wasn't prolific but all of us had certainly known when he was about to have something published. It all added to his charisma and standing, now he was offering us plebs the chance of the proverbial fifteen minutes of fame of which we should no doubt be grateful. It had shot Tradders down in flames and made him look as if it was he who doubted our collective integrity. Rambo and I both agreed that Tradders wasn't that type of guy, he just didn't want us lining up against each other even if it was for fun. Fun could get out of hand, competition for fun could go even further as had already been proven. Already myself, Rambo, Tom, Harry and Mike had cheated enough to get chucked out of the syndicate but as I said earlier the evil two of Tom and Harry had done enough to get chucked out twice and for all we knew Mike may have been with them on other prebaiting nights.

Rambo and I started wondering if anybody else in the syndicate was up to something to get their sticky mitts on the T.W.T.T. We started to lay odds. Tradders was 200-1 rank outsider but running a tight betting ship we were loathe to give any better odds. Tencher, although not being as clean cut as Tradders normally fished only for tench. If he was on six pound line it was hardly likely that he would bother to come up with some dastardly plot to get smashed up. He could get devious and fish for carp with eleven pound line and say he was fishing for tench and that was about as far as we reckoned it would go. Another 100-1 long shot. Dave and Tony were our naive novices. The Noddy boys. They had sussed the draw rigging so had motivation, but motivation is of little importance when you haven't much of a clue how to cheat in the first place. They didn't know enough and that seemed the top and bottom of it. We thought that maybe they might fish a snide rod on occasions (three was the maximum permitted) and they might even run to over flavouring their boilies, provided they were off shop-boughts. They were young and more prone to anarchy so we slashed their odds to Dave 25-1 and Tony 20-1. The discrepancy between them was on a whim of Rambo's, he thought that Tony was the more assertive of them and that this should be reflected in a five point difference.

Kipper Cole our glorious co-founder was an odd sort of bloke. He spent most of his time fishing asleep, not the most heinous action and not expressly conducive to cheating. However, I was not to be fooled and chalked him up at a sticky 10-1 as a dark horse.

"The bastard must be dreaming some good dreams to want to be akip so much and good dreams are usually naughty," I sagely explained to Rambo.

In the interest of amusement we decided to wipe the slate clean on those who had cheated so far and put down odds on them cheating again. Mike was even money, the least likely of our three enemies. Harry was 2-1 on and shithead Watt 100-1 on. That left the pair of us.

"Are you going to cheat again?" Rambo asked me.

"Well, I should think so. We're still down on the deal. I reckon Watt will cheat again, look at his odds. 100-1 on. Those bookies are pretty shrewd judges, they know the lay of the land, if he's going to cheat so am I. He started it, I'd be a fool not to. ....What about you then?"

"Course I am."

"Right," I said matter of factly, "no more bets on us two then."

Eventually Rambo left me to finish setting up. We had had a good laugh. I felt a deep affinity towards my collaborator. He was all right. Two months ago I wouldn't have hardly spoken to him, now we were kindred spirits against the common foe. What a sight for one of us to win the trophy and be in Carpworld, all written up by Watt the sad loser. That would hack him off so much he'd probably kill himself rather than write the article. I chuckled to myself at the very idea of it but the smile was short term as I considered the chances of either me or Rambo beating an angler of Watts ability. The smart money would be on Watt and he'd be odds on again. The odds on man against the odds stacked against man. Shit!

After Rambo had departed time passed slowly. I had everything ready by five and cooked myself a nice little meal of sausages and beans and had a cup of tea. I sat and waited for the off, happy to run the last few weeks events across my mind time and time again. Nobody came around to chat which was unusual, I could picture the other nine all waiting like myself but with even more excitement than usual as the game now had an extra external importance thrust upon it. At last at 11:45 the traditional rocket was fired into the air and with its incandescent explosion the season began. The rocket's launcher, Watt, was habitually a stickler for a midnight on the dot start. The premature start meant that even Ya Man himself was getting hot under the collar. He was anxious no doubt to get off to a cracking start and even more anxious to tell the carp magazine reading multitudes about it in his subtle self congratulatory prose. I cast my three baits out. Not if I had anything to do about it.

Chapter 5

At last the season had finally started and I was a fully paid up member of the Tom Watt Twenty Trophy, trying-to-attain-it, club. I sat on my bedchair a realistic and Kevin Maddocks endorsed six inches from the butt of my left hand rod. There was none of the old crashed out in the bivvy nonsense, this was serious. I sat with my arms folded, resolutely peering into the night at the three Optonics some four foot from my nose. My ears were ever expecting the cry of an agitated alarm. It was amazing how fishing with somebody else's bait had filled me to the brim with confidence. Rambo was the kiddie and I had the faith. If it had been at all possible by shear willpower or telekinesis, as the scientists like to call it, to physically make my indicators move I would have done. I focused on them not only with my eyes but also with my mind in a concentrated effort to score the opening goal in this nine month match.

After an hour my natural lack of fishing self-confidence insidiously started to worm its way back into my thoughts. Were all three rigs tangled? Had the boilies come off? Was I in the wrong spot? Even worse were Rambo and I totally in the wrong area? There was little that could be done if that was the case. Above all had Watt managed to catch one already, he rarely fished with his alarms turned up too loud so it wasn't obvious when he had caught. I think he done this so that he could get the pleasure of informing you personally that he had just had a twenty, especially when you had just replied in the negative to his unassuming question of your own success.

I guess fishing with low volume alarms is a personal thing. People consider that a tiny squeak is enough to let them know all they need to know. At night they use remote sounder boxes inside their bivvies so as not to disturb other anglers. Not us! Not on this occasion of the opening night of our dual effort to win the Tom Watt Twenty Trophy. We had decided to crank up to eleven as they say in the music business. This was to let each other know when we had a take and also, in the perfect world, to psychologically bludgeon our opponents into an inferiority complex as they were bombarded with the aural evidence of our supremacy. Nice theory and I remember sitting on my bedchair hoping it to become nice practise

I was tempted to use the radio that Rambo had given me, even though it was only one o'clock, but I was under orders only to use it when really necessary. I got up off my bedchair to have a stretch and a little walk. I paced around impatiently. I remember chastising my three alarms in aggressive whispers.

"Come on you bastards. Let's hear you scream. Now! Come on NOW!" They mocked me in mute amusement. I turned away from them and crawled into my bivvy wondering if I ought to move the bedchair in and start another sleepless, runless night at least under cover. Then it happened. The left hand, low tone (left-low, middle-middle, high-right) alarm banshee'd the night with a scream that had 'twenty' written all over it.

Now I don't know about all you guys but the sound of an active alarm has conditioned me with a sort of Pavlov's dogs' response. As soon as I hear that sound the old ticker goes promptly into overdrive and my adrenaline valves open up to full and flood my blood with the shaking chemical. This time it was the same only more so. I hit the run and with massive bemusement played in and landed a two pound tench in about thirty seconds flat. I was stunned. I put the tench back into its watery home and got on the radio to Rambo.

"Calling Rambo, over. Do you copy?" The reply was immediate. He had obviously heard the run and was waiting for info.

"Rambo here. What was it? Any size? Over."

"It was a fucking tench. No fucking size. Over." I exclaimed miserably. The reply was equally deflated.

"Oh Christ.......Jesus! If the bloody Tench are really on our bait we are in serious shit. You can kiss good-bye to the trophy, any hopes of getting that will be over. Over."

"Tell me about it," I said as I envisaged shoals of tench hoovering up our boilies before the carp were even aware of their existence. I thought of flogging the lot to Tencher cheap as a bulk buy. He probably wouldn't even want them because the bastard was cheating and fishing for carp.

Rambo's voice crackled through the radio again. "Look, let's get logical and rational about this. It's early days yet. Just cast out and re-bait. That tench might be the exception that proves the rule. Over."

Now sometimes people make statements in the heat of the moment that can be looked back upon as making about as much sense as a drunk nuclear physicist talking about chaos theory whilst trying to eat a quarter pounder in one mouthful. Thankfully this was not one of those occasions. I cast out again admittedly with my confidence dented but only a half hour later I heard what I hoped was Rambo's alarm. He was soon on the radio to say he had just had a fourteen, while he was relaying the good news a fish crashed out over the top of my open water baits. Things were looking up.

That first night will forever be engrained in my memory. Maybe it was because of the confidence shattering start that made the success that came after it all the more palatable. By nine in the morning I had had three doubles, one on each rod (I like to fish systematically!) the biggest being a shade under fifteen. Rambo had had just the one double but had knocked out four commons all about the nine pound mark in rapid succession. The elusive opening goal twenty was not to be had but it was now apparent that our bait was a good one, it seemed just a matter of time. Or was it as simple as that? Would Watt still be able to outfish us in twenty terms on a lower fish rate. I couldn't believe that on the first day morning he had caught more than either

Rambo or myself, however, his big fish captures were quite daunting to someone like myself. I wished that I could see what he was up to, but from the Bay West the Island itself blocked my view. I got onto the radio to ask Rambo if he had seen Watt have any action during daylight hours. With Rambo's binoculars it was likely that he could spy on Watt fairly easily and notice any sure signs of fish catching action.

"Calling Rambo. Do you copy Rambo? Over."

"Rambo here. What's on then? Had another? Over."

"No.... er, just asking if there was any action from Watt. Over."

"Yeah.... the shithead looks to have caught one that I've seen, at about six this morning. It looked a big fish. He weighed and photographed it and Kipper went round during the weigh-in, so I guess he could have been asked to witness a twenty. None of the others seem to have had much. Over and out."

This sounded bad news and Rambo's reading between the lines seemed spot on. For Kipper to move his fat arse off of a bedchair at six in the morning must have been because Watt had asked him. Getting Kipper to shift from his bedchair to which he seemed to be superglued and wake him up in the first place was no mean feat. About as difficult as catching a twenty in the first place, if it was a twenty. Inwardly I thought it would be. That would be bloody typical of Watt. He catches one fish and it's a twenty while we had eight between us and don't get within five pounds.

Catching the bigger fish has always seemed to be an odd thing. Some people seem to have an in-built ability to buck the simple rules of mathematical probability. If a water holds say, one hundred fish for round numbers and ten of them are twenties then in theory every tenth fish should be a twenty. You have a one in ten chance of catching one. Why is it then that you always seem to get one person who regularly betters the ratio? And why is it that the person who does, is as smug as a winning lottery ticket holder? Bloody obvious I suppose. It must be easy to let your ego run away with you when the rest of the field is still wading through the small commons and you're on your fifth twenty. This mystic ability, ('luck' some would call it, others 'skill' depending on your perspective or more likely on whether you were the one who was catching the twenties) would play a large part in deciding who would put their greasy mits on the T.W.T.T. The person who could get the best twenty/other fish ratio was more likely to win provided their catch rate was parable with the others.

Apart from individual ratio busting what else was there? Did certain areas produce bigger fish more readily? Possibly but I couldn't really see it on our water. Repeat captures, especially on a small water would definitely play a vital part of the overall scene. Last year there were ten different twenties caught and a good half a dozen or so in the eighteens and nineteens, maybe with all the illegal pre-season baiting that Watt and Harry had done over some considerable time we might have at a pinch, twenty twenties. If only it was possible to have a chat, Dr Doolittle style, to a twenty on the bank saying , 'now listen mate, if you let me catch you again..... you'll recognise the boilie, no problems? Yeah? Good. Well let's just say I'll see you right. No dieting though and if you get caught by somebody else I'll send the pike round to break your fins'. Such shenanigans of course are impossible. Carp are incorruptible and not easily threatened. They do as they do and not what you want them to. Maybe that's half the attraction of fishing.

The first morning went on. At eleven Tradders wandered up from the 1st Twenty swim to have a chat and ask me how things were going. I said that they were going well and I was a happy man, apart from what I thought Watt had caught which I neglected to tell him.

"You ought to be, all the bloody action you've been having," he said. "Your alarms kept rattling off, noisy things. What have you had? Every time they went off I thought,- Christ the sod's got another one."

I told him what I had caught and he nodded approvingly. The plan about cranking up the alarms had worked but it wasn't designed to get under Tradder's skin, only Watt, Harry and Mike's which now dawned on me as being stupid. How could I differentiate between pissing off the people I didn't care for and someone I did, like Tradders. Oh well this was war and there are always unjust casualties in war. Tradders himself had caught two fish, both single figures and he had lost a better fish when the hook had pulled. I asked him about the others. Apparently Tony was blanking like a good'un in the Pines but Harry had pulled out three fish from the Big Pads, fishing in real tight, of which one was a twenty four. Even more interestingly this fish was a known fish that had been one of the nineteens from last season. It was called Trigger, after a horse apparently. Kipper had named it, probably in his sleep, the moron. I wished the stupid fish had lived up to its namesake and pulled Harry in like a cart and drowned him in the pads.

Dave had caught a small mirror out of the Deep Corner and Tradders confirmed that Tom Watt superhero by royal appointment (himself) had caught just the one. Just the one twenty that is, but again a fish that wasn't a twenty last season. Kipper was still asleep in the Wide despite his one interruption for Watt's fish and Tencher was creating havoc in the Little Pads with the tench who were by all accounts being seduced by his flavoured sweetcorn. Mike had caught a low double from the Oak and was packing up to go home. Rambo had caught five but only one was a double. I had to stop myself from saying that I knew. I was amazed at the speed and accuracy at which the grapevine had gleaned all this information. How many cups of tea did you say that Watt had had? Pass the cyanide sugar down to him, there's a good chap.

Of all the info the one piece of news I couldn't get my head around was that Mike was packing up. Tradders had no idea why but concluded that he must have some important prior commitment. I remember thinking that it must be very important. Of course then I didn't know what I know now but all in good time reader, all in good time.

Tradders soon wandered back to his split cane rods and I was left to contemplate the meaning of life and generally study my own navel. By midday with no more action coming my way I drifted off into a comforting snooze brought on by lack of sleep and the sun's warming rays. Sometime later I was brought back to life by an Optonic, instinctively I flinched towards my rods but nothing was happening. As the fog of sleep cleared I realised that Rambo was in and stood and watched him land a fish after a dogged fifteen minute fight. It looked a good one as he lifted it from the water and I saw him beckon me over. I went to turn down my alarms and check the baitrunners were on. Strictly speaking I should have reeled in but you know how it is you don't want to. The baits had only been out between three and five hours and I didn't want to disturb anything so I left them.

I legged it round to Rambo as fast as I could praying that this was a fish that would trouble the scorer. By the time I got to his swim he had the fish in a weigh sling and was gazing at his 32lb Avons with a grimace on his face as bad as a bulldog licking cod-liver oil off a toilet seat. I got behind him and looked at the dial myself. The needle flickered resolutely on 19lb 14ozs.

"Have you zeroed them in properly?" I asked.

Rambo gave me a contemptuous look. I shrugged and looked down the bank towards the Oak. Mike had already gone. Maybe if he had still been there or more likely wandering up to have a quick shufty at the rig and bait my next idea wouldn't have materialised.

"Well done mate, your first twenty. Let's photograph her and put her back." Rambo gave me another look only this was more reflective. I spoke again. "Look both Harry and Watt have had twenties. Fuck it. It's close enough for my part, we don't want to get too far behind."

Rambo took one last glance at the scales and then put the sling down and went and got his camera. I took a couple of shots, one of each side and Rambo put the fish back.

As he knelt down by the waters edge and watched the fish disappear he said, "Nice fish that. Twenty pound two."

"Twenty pound four," I reminded him, "we don't want to cut it too fine otherwise some unscrupulous so and so might think we're cheating."

"True. We wouldn't want that." I laughed and started to walk back to my swim but turned back after a few yards. "Here. What bait did you catch that on, mate?"

"A Richworth tiger nut on a two foot pop-up."

"Really?"

"Really."

As I trudged back to the Bay West I had mixed emotions. Part of me felt really guilty about what the pair of us had just done but this was tempered by the manner in which Watt had conducted himself. Mingling with this was a feeling of elation of putting one over him and his cronies. It was the old chestnut of two wrongs making a right and by the time I was back to my rods I had convinced myself that the natural justice of our cheating to counteract their cheating was justified. The technicality of the fact that by doing so I lowered myself to their level and made the overall picture worse, I disregarded. I went to sort my rods out and put the alarms back on.

As I turned up the volume knob on the left hand alarm I suddenly noticed the line on the right hand rod was steaming out. I wound down and bent into a heavy fish. The line picked up out of the water and I looked out to see movement on the surface almost down to the Little Pads a 100 yards plus away from me. This had been a margin fished bait! With my hand clasped over the spool I turned the fish with a shit or bust manoeuvre, if it had got into the pads at that range I would have surely lost it. Slowly I played the fish back as it kited away from the pads and back into the bay. I tried to gain as much line as possible because I was conscious of picking up Rambo's open water bait as the fish came back up the bay and I was fortunate enough to avoid doing so.

Gradually I managed to get the fish within ten yards of the bank only it was way up in the end of the bay. I decided to walk down to the fish as far as I could rather than play it back to myself. I gained over half the distance between myself and the fish until I could get no further down the bank due to a bush. Side strain kept the fish out of the possible snags in the margins and soon the fish was rolling directly in front of me. I could see that it was a good mirror, my main problem, it suddenly dawned on me, was a severe lack of landing net which I had forgotten to take with me on my bankside walk-about. I cursed my stupidity. I looked over to Rambo hoping to get help but he wasn't by his rods. As I wondered where the hell he was and how the hell I was going to get my net he appeared around the side of the bush like a rabbit being plucked from a top hat. I was so surprised to see him that I think I physically jumped but luckily didn't pull the hook out!

Rambo loped down to my rods and bought the net back while I played the fish out. I can tell you that the old knees were knocking and the hands trembling. With every dive the tiring fish made my heart skipped a beat but all held firm and eventually its head came up and Rambo netted her. It looked a stone bonkers certain twenty.

"Brilliant, Rambo. Cheers," I said and boy did I mean it.

We went through the unhooking and weighing paraphernalia. This time there was no need to fiddle the weight. The fish was 25lb spot on. This fish was called Cyril, for no particular reason as far as I knew and had been a twenty last year when Tom 'legend in his own tackle box' Watt had caught it. It had a cluster of large scales just down from dorsal fin and was pretty much unmistakable. I was ecstatic. Cyril was a P.B for myself and the consequent photographs reflected this. After I had got Rambo to take pictures of either side, head on, either side on an angle, either side on another angle, head on from above and side on from below and above I gently put her back. Rambo complained that he had got a repetitive strain injury to his right forefinger and jabbed it sharply into my solar plexus just to prove it. Air rushed out from my lungs and I gasped to get it back.

"See, that should have pole-axed you. You're only doubled up. My finger's been weakened, I'm going to sue you for all the money you haven't got."

"As much as that," I wheezed.

Rambo smiled at me and slapped my shoulder. "Well done boy. That's a good fish you've had there. Keep it up. I can hear Watt's knees knocking from here. If we can keep the fish up here we've got a chance of pulling out a lead. Keep trickling the bait in and when the pair of us get low one of us can pop back to my flat and pick up a few more bags of boilies. Ok? I'll see you later."

"Thanks, Rambo. Good luck." I rasped hoarsely.

I cast back out, put out forty or so offerings and relaxed on my bedchair to contemplate the meaning of it all. What had just happened proved irrevocably that there was no justice or fair play in the world. If God existed he didn't give a shit about honesty and integrity being rewarded while deception and trickery were punished. You just did what you did and stood back and looked at the results. Me, Rambo, Watt and Harry all cheats. The rest honest as far as was known. Who had caught the most? The cheats. I had fiddled Rambo's fish to make it a twenty and walked back to my rods just in time to catch a fish which by rights should have been up to its gills in pads. Well in fact the bait shouldn't have even been in the water to catch the thing. I had cut a little corner by leaving my rods out and had been rewarded with a P.B. A better, more considerate angler would have pulled in and caught FA

It was all wrong. Leaving aside any possible damage that may have occurred to a fish through unsupervised rods there was the whole ethical problem of cheating the rest of the guys. They couldn't really compete against two groups whacking in the bait. We were literally stealing their fishing away from them, fishing that cost them hard earned cash. I thought deeper behind this sweeping generalisation to the people it effected. Watt, Harry and Mike, well fuck them. Tony and Dave, just boys, they could learn the hard way. Kipper, well he was hardly alive the amount of time he spent asleep, maybe he should stay awake and wise up a bit. Tencher, no feelings at all really and then Tradders the only guy who I did feel for. A genuine man who had been made to look a fool by Watt's sly speech in the car park. He had been right of course to wonder at the wisdom of the T.W.T.T, I only had to look at how I was behaving compared to last year when there wasn't a competition. It was plain to see what type of person I was turning into. It was all Watt's fault, he had started it the conniving whelp and Rambo and I were going to finish it, with him eating humble pie that had been cooked in a bath instead of a baking tin, there'd be so much of it. It was a case of the means justifying the ends and that was all there was to it.

For the rest of the afternoon I dozed fitfully. Inwardly I knew that I could live with the deeds that had been done and may be needed to be done in order to get one over Watt. When I awoke at about five I was drawn by movement over in the Oak swim. As my eyes focused and became accustomed to the still strong sunlight I made out the figure of Watt, rods and buzzer bars in hand settling into that swim. The cunning sod had walked past the normal points where bivvies were erected and was setting up, to be generous, on the very limits of what could still be considered the Oak swim. In fact I would have said that he was in fact past that boundary and was to all intents and purposes in the Bay East, Rambo's swim.

The conclusions to this were all too apparent. Despite having caught a twenty this was without doubt his only capture. Watt had either witnessed or heard of our success in the Bay and was trying to muscle in on the fish that were undoubtedly in the area and he'd been allowed to fish there by his good old buddy Mike vacating the swim. Only a man of very confident persuasion would have pushed the limits of what could correctly be called the Oak swim by virtue of a topological definition. When Watt pushed his buzzer bars in terra-firma he was only 15 to 20 yards from Rambo. He shoved them in with the air of some colonial explorer staking claim to a vast tract of land, thing was, had he considered the restless nature of the natives?

Watt returned to his original swim the Island (how chuffed I felt that the swim he had conned had not been that successful) to get the rest of his gear. While he was gone Rambo nipped down and moved his buzzer bars back another twenty yards, no doubt in a friendly gesture so that he had less distance to walk! On his return Watt paused at his rods, made a decision and took his bedchair and rod holdall back to the original Oak/Bay East position. Again he returned to the Island for his bivvy and again Rambo moved the bedchair and rod holdall back to where he had put the rods. It was brilliant to watch. I could imagine them being there for years, Watt shifting gear up only for Rambo to shift it back. It was sure fire that Watt couldn't shift gear as fast as Rambo and I reckoned that it wouldn't take too many more attempts by Watt before he himself was shifted, probably into the middle of next week, by Rambo's right fist.

When Watt returned with bivvy he sensibly put it down with the rest of his tackle. His body language was that of defiance, he stood bolt upright, both hands on hips looking at his gear and shaking his head. After this little display he strode purposefully up the bank in large positive strides to where Rambo was sitting legs stretched out on his bedchair. Watt stood over him and started to talk, wagging a threatening finger. This speech seemed to last ages, a good three or four minutes. Rambo, unimpressed, remained passively seated until Watt appeared to have finished, he then sprung from his bedchair and stood virtually Adam's apple to nose with Watt. From this lofty position of tactical advantage Rambo spoke waving his arm back down the bank. It was only one sentence. Watt's stature seemed to wither from its already vertically challenged beginning, his body crumpled and shoulders rounded, like a dog with its tail between its legs he turned and shuffled down the bank. Needless to say he started to set up where Rambo had put his gear.

I quickly went into my bivvy and got on the radio. "Rambo, come in Rambo. Do you copy? Over."

"Rambo here. Over."

"What happened between you and superjerk?" I blustered excitedly. I heard nothing and then realised. "Over." I added an octave above my normal voice.

Rambo answered in a malevolent sneer. "Oh the pompous sod started coming the old acid about how I shouldn't be touching his personal property, that he was merely looking to utilise the lake to its maximum potential, that he had no desire to upset myself or impose himself, that he would respect my left hand rods rightful claim to territory and would not impinge upon it, that he had always regarded the spot he wanted to fish as part of the Oak swim. Oh God he rambled on for ever. I just told him to shut the fuck up, fish where I'd put his gear or I'd smash his face in. I told him he was just trying to pounce my fish off of me and if roles were reversed he'd be the first to moan. I think he got the message. Over"

    I agreed with Rambo, he certainly had. Here we were not twenty-four hours into the season and things were hotting up nicely. The scores on the doors were Watt one, Harry one, Rambo one, yours truly one, the rest still in the starting stalls. All to play for as they say, all to play for.

Chapter 6

At nine in the evening on that first day of the season Watt came round to see me. After failing to blatantly muscle in on the fish in the Bay area and the seeing off delivered to him by Rambo, I would have expected him to be downbeat. Added to this was the fact that the pair of us had taken another fish each, neither a salt rubbing in twenty unfortunately, but more success nevertheless while Watt had had nothing. Of course I had underestimated the resistance of his ego to such dents and knew pretty soon into the conversation that the sly bastard was trying to pump me more than a boat fisherman might pump a huge skate to the surface. Only much more surreptitiously.

"Hello, Matt. How are you doing?" He asked in a calm, generous voice that oozed friendship. I felt my head twitch involuntarily and tried to calm myself and hide my dislike for him.

"All right." It came out rather curt.

"Good," he said revealing no rebuff. "Just had another one, then?"

"Yeah. A mirror just over twelve," I said matter of factly.

"Ummm. I'm just having a quick walk round and chat to everyone actually. You and Rambo are the last two to see as I walked round the other way from where I'm fishing. I'm getting the Tom Watt Twenty Log up to date before I cast out for the night and I'm making a few notes for my articles at the same time.. As you've done so well you'll definitely be in the first one." He paused to let me say 'great'. I could play at charades.

"Great," I said with as much enthusiasm and as little sarcasm as I could muster. He looked at me a bit longer than he would normally. I cursed inwardly, I must act as I would have done before I knew what a shithead this man was. Last season I would have felt gratified that he was even speaking to me, a man of his fishing calibre, but that was all dead and buried now. Awe had been replaced by something between disgust and loathing.

"Yes, it should be an excellent article with all you guys doing so well and catching. It makes it so much easier to write good prose when there's lots of action to describe especially when it isn't purely about oneself. Of course I have written articles about myself solely and the fish I've caught, good fish as well, thirties that sort of size but I think the average carp angler will be able to relate easier to the situation we have here." I nodded. "Now then," Watt continued opening up a large hardback book, "have you had a twenty yet?"

"Oh yes." I said, "I had Cyril at spot on 25lb earlier on. My best ever."

"You're best ever at 25?" (Slight condescending amusement). "Well, well done. Well done indeed. Let me just enter that into the log." He noted it down while I wished he would just get out of my face before I tried to garrotte him with some 15lb Big Game line.

"Who witnessed that for you?" Watt asked.

"Rambo did."

"Ahh. Rambo. Our strange companion." Watt smiled as he noted this little nugget of information down as well.

"I witnessed a twenty for him as well. He had that one just before mine." A frown flickered across Watt's face before he could help it. "20lb 4ozs that was."

"Indeed. He had set the scales properly I take it? I don't doubt Rambo it's just that he is such a strange lad. We even had an altercation when I moved into the Oak swim, he seemed to think I was crowding him. What with that and his behaviour at the draw for the first day swims one wonders how much grip he's got on reality."

"Well, it all looked pukka to me." I said coolly avoiding any arguments. "I didn't exactly send his scales off to the Weights and Measures Department but they said 20lb 4 and that was good enough for me."

"Yes, quite. I'll enter that in the log then. There. Four of us share the lead. Harry has the other twenty capture along with myself. Yes my fish was 23 - 10, I was very pleased with that fish first time out with my new bait." The whiff of deceit wafted up my nose and being the skate I mentioned earlier I got ready to hug the bottom . "I thought I'd use a fishmeal this year only flavour it with something sweet. Mega tutti-frutti actually, with a sweetener," Watt bent the rod double, "I don't know what the likes of you or Rambo are using but it will be interesting to see if your baits can keep up with mine."

"I'd have thought it was the other way round at the moment," I said indignantly.

Watt smiled benignly and wagged a non aggressive finger. "Early days yet young man, you were lucky to fall on the fish."

'Yes. Must have been a bit disappointing drawing the hot swim and it not producing. After all the trouble you went to get it.' I wanted to add.

"Still lucky for you your friend Mike moved out to let you up here. How much did you pay him?" I asked with innocent cheek but I was beginning to lose my rag.

Watt's reaction surprised me. "Yes, ha-ha very good. I, er, I really am at a loss as to why Mike left so early. Very strange, very strange but don't look a gift horse etc." I was convinced that he really was put out about Mike but he dismissed it as it was to his benefit.

Watt tried again. "Have you been putting much bait out?"

"Nah, not really," I lied, my big wing like fins gratefully touching sand.

"I'm putting about 30 offerings around each hookbait and perhaps a few more before I cast out before nightfall. I'm fishing two bottom baits and one on a pop-up. I had the twenty on the pop-up and I might start to fish two rods on a pop-up. Two pop-ups in the margins as I had my fish in the margins."

"Yeah," I said, "good idea."

Watt smiled and decided that he would just give up, cut the line and head for shore. "Anyway, I must be off. Good luck."

"Yeah, cheers. You too." Bastard! Watt left me to my own thoughts. He had tried to trade information by magnanimously offering snippets from his own store first. I guess in the past I would have been so overwhelmed to be talking tactics and bait with the great Tom Watt, so proud to actually be asked my opinions that I would have spouted the lot, but this time he got diddly-squat. Just like you reader, if our bait was similar to Watt's or totally different is not for me to say. Sorry.

That night I felt confident of action but apart from a liner on my right hand rod nothing happened. I was pretty sure that Rambo had got one in the dark but I wasn't called to witness the event. The next day was very hot and the fish cruised aimlessly on the top. I half-heartedly put one rod out on the surface but with no success. I didn't make contact with Rambo due to Watt's close proximity as I didn't want to give away our partnership. I wanted to tell him that Watt was feeling the pressure a bit and gloat with Rambo over the way I had stonewalled him, but it would have to wait.

At midday Tradders came round to tell me that Kipper and Dave had had a stand up row when both of them had tried to move into the Island (Watt's previous swim) at the same time. Apparently it was nearly wet weigh slings at seven paces until Dave made way by virtue of seniority. Kipper moved into the Island, meticulously set up and cast out with millimetre accuracy only to fall asleep and lose a fish that snagged itself in the margin branches of the Island because the silly old sod had been waylaid by an obstinate sleeping bag zip. What he was doing in a sleeping bag on the hottest day of year defies all logic but then again logic and Kipper are alien to each other. Tony had wound in, moved into Dave's first day draw swim and commiserated with his best mate by drinking tea with him for three hours after the fracas. It was deep gloom in the Deep Corner.

Harry was still having some action but was having to cast in really tight to the pads to get pick ups and was consequently losing as many as he was landing. His last take, an hour after first light, had happened just as he stepped up to a bush, member in hand to have a leak. From the 1st Twenty, Tradders had seen the unequal battle between Harry, a half emptied bladder, dripping penis and a well embedded carp. The carp had slipped the hook and Harry had pissed his trousers. If only I could have witnessed it, it couldn't have happened to a nicer bloke.

Cheered up by Harry's misfortune and the fact that Watt was having as little action as me or Rambo the hot day seemed to drag slightly less. At that time there were just the four twenty fish out. Would one of us nudge ahead or would somebody else wade into the foray with a fish to trouble Tom's Twenty Log Book. Captain's Log: Star Date 17th of June. What a strange world this is, these men seem besotted with their quest to catch this odd marine life called 'the carp'. They wait for days on end, ever vigilant they sit by their equipment with which they catch these blessed creatures. These strange beings have no concept of time, they are diverted from all else by their singular pursuit. IT IS SO BORING to watch them. Maybe we could learn from them but frankly..... who cares? Beam me up, Scotty I've had a gutful.

Ahead warp factor 2. (Try and do the voice when you read this, it makes it so much better).

By evening the fish had dropped from the surface and it had clouded over and was much cooler. This looked more promising. I was thinking that indeed it was more promising when I had a belter on my left hand rod which had been margin fished up into the bay. As I struck into the fish I glanced over at Watt who I knew would be watching me. 'Eat shit', I thought and then ate it myself as the hook pulled.

Half an hour later the same rod went again only this time all held nicely. I netted the fish myself fairly sharpish as luckily it had picked up the bait and bolted up the margin towards me. It was obviously a low IQ fish but pounds and ounces cut more ice than Mensa numbers when you're head to head in competition. The mirror was a hefty old lump and with the usual lack of manual dexterity I managed to unhook her and get her in the sling to be weighed. Ding-dong calling Avons! Around once eight pounds, and again sixteen, past sixteen and into the green ha-ha! The colour Watt was surely going. Ever onward clockwise, around past the six o'clock mark and stop at ....21lb 5ozs. I was in the lead. In fact I had caught twice as many twenties as the next best, that meant at that moment I was twice as good at carp fishing as Watt (you can prove anything with statistics and a bucketful of self delusion).

Wary of implicating myself with Rambo I bellowed out to Watt that I had just caught a twenty and would he get his fat arse around to my swim a bit rapid and witness it for me. Well in a politer form anyway. As God's gift to carp fishing walked around to see me I had a brainwave. If only I had them with me. Quickly I rummaged around in my wax cotton coat's pockets. Tucked away in the right hand pocket were a couple of shelf life baits that I had been using in March of last season. I know it's sad but I didn't have a bait that was working and the convenience of not spending time making bloody boilies that you had no confidence in had turned me towards a bag of Richworth Streamselect Tropicanos. Their shelf life capacity was living up to high standards, the boilie looked as new. Quickly I took off my bait and hair-rigged the Tropicano after giving it a smart dunking in the lake.

Had a boilie ever been used for such a subversive reason? I carefully laid out my bog standard bolt rig in the landing net so that it looked just as if I had unhooked a fish and left it. I had a boilie acting as a kind of double agent, a substitute, a dubious doppelganger. It was a plant, a red herring, a signpost in the road rotated 180 degrees, above all it was a trick Tropicano. My rig had caught a twenty, would it catch Watt? It was role reversal time, he had tried to pump me now I was going to try and catch him. Soon enough the big-headed buffoon arrived, all enthusiastic and congratulatory. He checked the weight and photographed the fish and put it back for me, he even told me the last time he caught it but it hadn't been a twenty then. Poor sod. During all this helpful bonhomie I had watched Watt's beady, artful eyes glance at my rig and now with everything completed he kindly untangled my rig from the keepnet mesh, lifted it clear and held bomb and boilie in separate hands. I could hear the Optonic going off.

"Hmm, I see you're using a shortish hooklength then?" No you moron you're just short-sighted, it's a 2ft confidence rig.

"Yeah."

"Is that a shop bought boilie, it's so perfectly round?" Hook set and play the bastard in.

I couldn't tell a lie. "Yeah, it's a Streamselect Tropicano actually."

"And you've had all your takes on that type of boilie?" Asked Watt with casual indifference. He didn't fool me.

"Yep. Every one." I could tell a lie.

"Hmm interesting. Oh well must get back, well done."

"Thanks, Tom." Landed and banked, sucked in and spat out.

I couldn't exactly see Watt stopping using his own bait and rushing down to the local tackle shop to buy them out of Tropicanos but it might confuse him and throw him down a blind alley. It would certainly give him something to think about and it had given me a rush to fool him.

That night Rambo caught his second twenty and asked Watt to witness that as well. It was brilliant making him eat shit like this. I also had another double and Rambo a single figured common just before dawn. All the fish were caught on the rods that were up into the bay. Our bait that had been constantly fed in was doing its job of holding the fish in the area. Even though Watt had edged his right hand rod as far up as he dare without running the risk of a diet change from shit to Rambo knuckle sandwich he was blanking out. He just couldn't get on the fish. Fish must have been moving in and out of the bay to some extent because I was getting liners on my other rods but they didn't seem to be feeding elsewhere as readily as in the bay and on our bait. Was the bait so good that it was a case preoccupation already? I hoped but couldn't believe it.

After the night, day three (the 18th) passed with a fish each for Rambo and myself. What with all the takes and keeping the bait going in I was running short of boilies, by the afternoon I only had two or three hundred left.

About this time Watt had reeled in and gone around the lake, I had rushed around to Tradder's swim to watch Watt deep in conversation with Harry and had then shot back to have a parlez with Rambo. We both told each other of all the latest happenings and confirmed what we had caught, in five minutes we were both up to date with each others knowledge. Rambo's second twenty had been a smidgen over 23lb and had pleased him greatly but not as much as my bogus boilie scam. That had really tickled him much like it had tickled Watt, the fat old trout.

Mind you, it wasn't all laughter and light, Rambo was nearly out of boilies as well. One of us would have to go back to his flat to pick up the remaining few thousand. Rambo had foreseen this problem but had reckoned on the bait we had originally brought lasting another day or so longer. He hadn't wanted to bring the lot because he was concerned that given the hot weather that had been forecast (of which we had had only one day) the boilies might spoil. In any case it was no big deal to pop back and get them, it was just a case of somebody doing it and missing a few hours fishing. The few hours that you would undoubtedly catch the fish of a lifetime of course. I felt it was down to me to go back for them so I took Rambo's flat key and went back to my swim.

It was about four o'clock by then so I decided to reel in straight away and tidy my gear up. I tucked everything away from any prying eyes and ambled around past Rambo again, up the path and back to the car park. I decided to go home have a shower, get a take-away and then go to Rambo's flat and get back to the lake by about six and hopefully catch the evening feeding spell that had produced the lost fish and the 21lb 5.

I got in my van and drove off at a relaxed pace. As I got into the outskirts of my town I came to a roundabout, I had to wait to give way to some traffic that was coming from my right and casually eyed the drivers that went in front of me until suddenly, oblivious to my existence, I saw Mike. Something inside me was troubled and for some reason of which I am not sure of until this day I followed him. As luck would have it two more cars had got between myself and Mike and I could therefore chase him comfortably without little fear of detection. We drove on for five or so minutes, I knew where Mike lived although I had never been to his house and we were certainly not going there. I nearly lost him at a junction but soon caught up, there was nobody between us now and I slowed my pace to be less obtrusive. A few more turns and I was pretty sure where we were going. A final left brought Mike into the road where Tom Watt lived. I parked up right at the top of the road which was some 400 yards from Watt's house. I had been to see him there when I had originally joined the syndicate and could remember the rather plush four bedroomed detached property quite well.

I could also remember Watt's wife quite well. Although Tom was a healthy bloke he was one of those persons of whom it is difficult to judge their age. He could have been anything from 40 to early 50's whereas his wife was a very trim attractive woman of about 35-ish. I wondered at the time what an attractive person like her was doing with a bloke like Tom. Perhaps she had been conned by his charm and intelligence like I had or more likely by the comfortable lifestyle he could afford her. They say love is blind except when it comes to eyeing up the bank balance, then it gets remarkably sure sighted.

I cautiously walked down towards the Watt residence. The road was fairly empty of parked vehicles and I could not see Mike's car where it should have been if he was going where I thought he was going. I stopped and looked harder, suddenly right at the end of the road Mike appeared from a side street. He had done exactly the same as me. I had done it to avoid detection, why had he? I snapped out of my deliberations and ducked behind a wall occasionally checking up on Mike's progress. Sure enough he went into Watt's house.

Double dilemma! What to do? Intrigue overcame fear and I walked down to Watt's house and taking my life in my hands darted down the side path, through the open gate to the back corner of the house. From that corner there was some four foot of brickwork before the patio door that lead from the patio into the lounge. The window I had run past at the front was the small study where Watt had his writing paraphernalia and fishing books. He had been most keen to impress me with that particular room which was adorned, Rambo-style, with pictures of himself holding large carp. I leant against the brickwork, my heart banging and nerves fraying. This gut churning sensation was one that was beginning to become all too familiar what with recent events, much more of this and I would become an adrenaline junkie.

It dawned on me that now I was here in this ludicrous position I might as well look to see if I could find out what was occurring. I edged my way along the four foot of oh so lovely, not-transparent-at-all-brickwork right to the door. It was then that I nearly had a coronary as Mrs Watt, Jennifer, if I remember correctly, swished the curtains across the door just as I was about to have a sneak look into the lounge. It frightened the life out of me but I remained undetected. I bravely walked to the middle of the door and was rewarded. The curtains, pulled in such haste had a tiny gap that any pathetic voyeur, such as myself, could look through.

I peered in with an eager eye to see Jennifer and Mike pulling their kit off of each other like a couple of dogs ripping apart an old bedspread. This was high passion indeed! Soon, both in their birthday suites the pair of them put on a show that would have cost me about twenty quid in the red light district of Amsterdam. They were all over each other, there wasn't a redundant orifice in sight and the coffee table was made of sterner stuff than you would have originally imagined. To be fair I was impressed. Mike acquitted himself fairly well but then again who was to say that he hadn't cheated by abusing himself an hour or so earlier thus prolonging the agony so to speak, but let's not be churlish about such matters. All this before me explained why he wasn't at the prebaiting night with Tom and Harry and it explained why he packed up early, not to help put Watt on the fish as I had thought but to have easy access to some serious shagging with his wife. The cunning whelp!

What I had just witnessed gave me a lever on Mike as long as a barge pole and the fulcrum, not to put too fine a point on it, was his bollocks. It was a trump card ready and waiting to be unleashed, it made any aces Tom had look pretty sickly by comparison. All I had to do was determine the best time to play it.

With all this in mind I made fast back to my van unnoticed by any nosey neighbour as far as I could tell. From there I called at Rambo's and picked up the boilies. I must admit there was a certain temptation to have a quick rummage for any skeletons or otherwise but I erred on the side of caution, Rambo had probably stuck a human hair across every opening cupboard and door to detect such duplicity. In any case he might have wired up some hideous booby trap as well that would have blown me to smithereens. All in all it wasn't worth it, besides we were a team, albeit a lopsided one, me being more ballast than anything, but my new info improved my standing no end and gave more power to our collective elbows.

After getting the boilies I went to get my take-away which I ate in the van and from there I went home for my shower. The house was empty so I left a note for Sophie saying everything was going well and I would see her later on. The detour to Watt's house had made me later than expected and it wasn't until about half six that I got back to the lakes' car park. I walked briskly down the path, past Kipper on the Island who to my complete amazement was actually awake. The old codger was making himself a meal after being surgically removed from his lounger. I wondered whether Kipper was in fact the surviving child of a pair of Siamese twins and missed the close physical contact of another body and, unable to convince any human or animal, had settled for a bedchair. Or rather settled on one and now had great difficulty in getting off the bloody thing. I left him to his gourmet delight after a brief greeting. I passed Tencher who was opening up his millionth tin of sweetcorn and wandered around to the Oak where Watt was sitting glued to his rods. As I got near to him he turned and smiled at me. I smiled back thinking that I knew something that he didn't and he wasn't as clever as he thought.

"All right then, Tom." By the way, do you know who's knocking your missus off? I added to myself.

"Oh yes. Very all right young man. It seems that you picked an inopportune time to leave the lake."

Alarm bells and at high decibels. "Ohh?"

"Indeed. Since your departure I have edged into the lead. Two twenties in two hours, not bad eh?"

Oh bugger! "Really...." Stunned reaction. Hopeful question. "Did... Umm Rambo have anything while I was gone?"

"Oh no," said Watt smugly, "just my two although Rambo witnessed them. I think it stressed him out a bit you know. After the second one I said to him that maybe if I had fished where I wanted I might not have caught. So I thanked him for moving my gear back down. I told him that he must have known the fish were going to move out the bay soon. Naturally I only said it as a bit of fun but it seemed to upset him somewhat."

I bet it did. Watt must be the luckiest man out (apart from having an unfaithful wife) but to catch two twenties in two hours and rip the piss out of Rambo and still be alive. I left Watt and came to a seething Rambo. I gave him his share of the boilies, he snatched them from me without thanks. Boy was he niggled, not just by Watt but the seeming injustice of it. There was Watt doing his level best to muscle in on our sport, he gets told to hoof it and then low and behold everything turns turtle, some fish move out and bingo! The jammy git's in position A1 to reap the benefit.

Some i.e. Watt would call it good fishing, Rambo was calling it something else. Now it was a case of wait and see as to whether it was time to think about quitting the bay. The pendulum had well and truly swung. The pair of us felt frustrated. That's the thing about fishing there are times when you are limited to what you can do about certain situations. If it had been a game of football that we were playing we could have tried many tactics to get back our lead or at least get our own back with a few crunching tackles for example. A nice over the top shin ripper on Watt the midfield general and an elbow in the temple for Harry the tricky forward. Mike would have been taking an early bath with the captain of the ladies team and could only be got at by slipping bromide in his half-time cup of tea. Of course it wasn't that easy, this was a different situation. All we could do was fish on and see what happened.

I left Rambo to pull his hair out. I had not told him about Mike because I wanted to share my hard earned information at a better time, a time when Rambo wasn't constantly smashing his fist into his unhooking mat. I also neglected to mention bankside etiquette and how it was understood that unusual vibrations could spook carp. Vibrations like human fist pile-driving and suchlike. All in all I cut a slightly dejected figure as I traipsed around to my Bay West swim. When I got there Dave and Tony were waiting for me. Together the pair of them had whipped themselves up into self-righteous indignation brought on by Dave's conflict with Kipper over the Island swim which had in turn raked the smouldering coals of the first day draw fiddle by the unholy trinity of Tom, Harry and Mike. The pair of them wanted to take some action, they felt belittled and cheated. I knew the feeling and out of weariness, sheer spite and some guilt about how rude I had been to Dave in the car park, I told them of Mike and Jennifer. I had given them the dynamite, it was up to them how, when and where they chose to explode it.

Chapter 7

That night (the 4th night of the season that welcomed the dawning of the 19th of June) was a poor one for myself, Rambo and Watt. Forgetting the fact that we all blanked, I was personally traumatised about the wisdom of passing on my amazing information about Jennifer and Mike to both Dave and Tony. Rambo had spent a night wringing Watt's neck in his cold sweat dreams and Watt himself had undoubtedly had an untroubled night unaware of the impending nuclear explosion coming his way. 'Always the last to know' is the expression and song as well if I remember rightly, if it was to ring true in Tom Ya Man's case rested with myself and the terrible twosome. By morning I had convinced myself that spilling the beans about Mike spilling his seed had been a clever move. Although I had released my lever to a certain extent it might let me get on with the task in hand of catching more twenties than Watt while others became embroiled in some horrendous mud slinging and underhand action that was bound not to be conducive to successful fishing. (Excuse me reader while I wipe away a tear of mirth caused by that last mega-understatement).

Rambo came to see me at about six in the morning. It looked as if it was going to be another hot, sunny day, Rambo was already in a T shirt that had the legend 'Fuck Off' emblazoned on the back and front. I could just tell that he was still in a bad mood and so tried to cheer him. I told him all about the little incident I had witnessed the day before. If I was ever in any doubt about the therapeutic value of telling a tale of misfortune, misfortune falling upon a disliked individual, the broad smile on Rambo's face dispelled it. He was chuffed. He was less ecstatic, as I had imagined, about me having told Dave and Tony but he reckoned that I had found out the information and was at liberty to do with it what I liked.

"I just wish that you had told me first." He had said. "I think I would have tried to persuade you to keep it a secret until we decided the optimum moment for using it, but, what the hell it may well work out as you say. The others may be distracted by it but I'm sure that it will eventually come out that you were the person who found out about it and suck you into the shenanigans then. Still, your choice, mate, your choice."

"I would have told you but you were a bit irritated last night." I said not wanting him to think I'd rowed him out.

"Was I! Christ I was fuming! No! Forget I said it. You did well to have the gumption to do what you did. Have a gold star." He laughed. I wasn't going to get bollocked after all.

We carried on talking about fishing strategy. The theory from Rambo was that we had succeeded in holding the fish in the bay which had been the main feeding area for some reason or another, partly our bait and partly that indefinable element, carp free-will. He now thought that the fish had moved out at the very minute I was gawping at my free sex show and snake-bite Watt had pulled out a couple of twenties as they did (big fish busting ratio, see earlier) on the strength of his prebaiting. With a three way blank last night the bay was now looking to be hard graft. There was precious little movement at the moment and we had had no line bites or anything. It seemed fair enough to assume that we would struggle from now on although it was too early to be sure. We had gone periods of inaction and then caught again but Rambo said that the tea leaves read different.

Due to the fact that we had nine members still fishing it was difficult to move. Watt had moved into the Oak that Mike had left for nookie, Kipper having outranked Dave had gone into the Island where Watt had been and so the vacant swim was the Wide, Kipper's draw swim, the one immediately right of the Island. It was an indifferent swim with no features as traditionally the Island hot spot was centre and right tip therefore you had no chance of fishing against the Island from the Wide swim. At a pinch you might occasionally be able to fish the left hand pads of the Little Pads swim (the swim to the right of the Wide) but again 99% of the time the person in the Little Pads would have a bait in that spot. All in all it was clear that the pair of us would have to sit it out and wait for a few people to decide that they had had enough and then move to the best that was available.

Harry seemed to have the best chance of doing well. He was on an introduced bait and with a fair number of fish coming out of the bay, his swim along with the Island were certain to get visited by fish and in course give some action. At least Watt had burnt his bridges by coming out of the Island but it had to be said that it had been a move worth doing even if it had been dead fluky. He had moved and had caught two twenties, end of story.

Rambo left me to have a brew and cook breakfast. Watt had remained snuggled up in his bivvy all during our analysing session and hopefully remained unaware of our liaison. When he did awake he promptly reeled in and moved all his gear down into the Wide swim. One other person seemed to agree with our interpretation of events. I couldn't stop myself thinking that we must be right because Watt thought the same thing. Old habits of respect for someone's fishing ability die slowly.

I wondered where the sly old fox was going to fish in the Wide swim, I should have realised it wouldn't be as simple as that. The answer was not so much in the Wide swim but more from it, onto the hot spot off the right tip of the Island. Apparently, I later discovered, he had had a long chat with Kipper who, undoubtedly in a mental state of confusion from being awoken so early and from being kept awake so long, had allowed him free access to the best spot in his swim. The stupid bastard. Tencher had told me all this as he was right next to it all in the Little Pads. What could you do? If Kipper was dumb enough to let Tom cast over into his swim, into a well know patrol route feeding spot, then what could anybody else say or do about it? If Kipper, the person it most concerned was happy, how could any of us claim to be dissatisfied about it? At a stretch you could shout foul and claim team tactics but Kipper wasn't part of Watt's team. He was just the co-founder along with Watt who was obviously still influenced by his persuasive tongue. Watt had done us again.

It was around this time, about eight in the morning while Tencher was still with me telling me about Watt's smart move that I heard the commotion from the far side of the lake. It came from the Big Pads and treachery had been at work at night. Harry was going apeshit, effing and blinding at the top of his voice and when we had run round to Tradder's swim we could see him picking things up so that he could throw them as hard as he could back down to the ground.

The three of us Tencher, Tradders and myself peered into the distance and watched Harry run round in little circles shouting 'fucking hell' at top volume fairly regularly, once every three seconds, and generally sling his gear around. First he picked up his bedchair and threw that down, then he got hold of his large water bottle and threw that down. Once was obviously not enough so he picked it up again, right above his head and threw it down again. It split. This agitated him even more, if that was possible, so he kicked it as hard as he could. Unfortunately for him the rupture had been insufficient to let all the water out and he had nearly broken his toe. Further incensed he hobbled back to the bedchair, shouted 'fucking hell' for good measure and picked it up and hurled it to the ground again.

"He's not happy is he," said Tradders with a tinge of mockery.

He certainly wasn't. The landing net had just been launched, javelin-like into a rhodie bush and his coat had been subjected to a rather poorly choreographed war dance. Now he was on his hands and knees pummelling the ground with both like a small child having a no-sweeties-for-you tantrum.

Rambo arrived. "What the bloody hell's going on?"

"Harry's running amok," said Tradders matter-of-factly, "either something or somebody has upset him or his brain has addled."

"Something must have upset him then, he hasn't got a brain," said Rambo dryly.

"He won't have any tackle let alone a brain if he carries on at this rate," I said watching the graceful arc of a flying rig bin followed by three Optonic pouches burying themselves in the rhodie bush. Much more of this and the rhodie bush would be able to set up as a tackle retailer.

"What on earth is he doing now?" asked Tencher.

Harry was now standing with arms and legs spread-eagled, shaking his two fists heavenward screaming that ever pertinent question 'who the fucking hell did this' upward at the sky. The 'this' appeared to be something dangling from his hands. Ever ready Rambo studied the scene through his binoculars.

"Hmm. I would say that Harry is holding the two ends of some sounder-box cables. Neither end has jack plugs." Rambo pulled the binoculars away from his eyes as we all turned to look at him. "I would say boys, that dear old Harry has had his alarm to sounder box cables cut. Not unless this lake and surrounding woodland has some kind of rare wire chewing beaver it would be safe to say that he has been wilfully sabotaged."

And he had. The rare Sussex wire chewing beaver was declared innocent by virtue of the clean cut on the cables. I wanted to say that it could have been the work of the even rarer Sussex wire cutting opposable thumbed in possession of snips beaver, but didn't. Harry's frustration had been doubled, well trebled actually, by the fact that it appeared that he had lost three runs. The line was gone and the monkey climbers had been held in the position that Harry had left them by the small rubber band that stops them falling off the stick. He had first noticed a lack of line after going for a morning piddle. What with the lost fish last time he had gone for a leak, I dubbed Harry the 'The Piddley Problem Man' but not to his face.

Naturally Watt called the lot of us around to Harry's swim to explain what had happened. All Harry could say was that it had happened between his twilight cast the night before and about eight in the morning and could someone let him have some water for a cuppa. Evidently all that shouting had made him a bit hoarse and he had weakly added that his own supply had drained into the ground. That really creased me and it was a struggle not to laugh. Both Dave and Tony (Deep corner and Pines, the two swims either side of Harry) said that they had heard or seen nobody, although as they said they could have been soundly asleep.

In the end after a little introspective navel gazing the episode was put down to kids playing a nasty little joke. The members decided that they weren't the type of people to do such things (no comment) and outsiders in the form of children were the logical scapegoats. We often had the farmer's grandchildren walk by the lake with their friends, they knew the area well enough to move about at night and the Big Pads was the swim that was closest to the farmhouse. Several members noted the often yobbish behaviour by the kids which was fair comment, they had plenty of mouth like most kids have today. In the end the self righteousness or deviousness of the S.S kangaroo court managed to convince themselves of external foul play. Our beloved syndicate leader warned us to be vigilante and that at the next opportunity he would have a word with the farmer about this 'disgraceful incident'. It was all so plausible but knowing what I knew convinced me the enemy lay within.

As we all sidled off back to our swims I decided to linger and offer a few insincere platitudes of condolence to Harry. After that I shuffled off to have a little word with Tony now that he was alone in the Pines.

"I can't believe that happened to Harry you know." I said by way of an opening gambit.

Tony gave me a level stare. "The others might say that but you should know better."

"What d' you mean?" I said knowing full well what he meant.

"Well, Harry has just got his comeuppance for fiddling the draw. Watt has yet to pay, so has Mike."

"So you did it, then?" I said, like some B movie gumshoe who was wired.

"Yep. Revenge, simple as that. Dave and I did it at two in the morning. What really breaks me up is that the pretentious wanker thinks he lost three fish. Look." Tony showed me into his bivvy and pulled out three rigs still connected to a mass of mainline. "Even Dave and I aren't Noddy enough to let fish suffer. After we outed the alarms we just bit through the lines and pulled in all three baits hand over hand. If he only thought about it, it would be obvious that he hadn't got snapped up by fish. I mean, did he really think that the carp moved the indicator bands so as they looked the same height as he had left them? Dickhead! We only did that so that if he glanced out from his bivvy he wouldn't have noticed anything untoward. Here, see what boilie he's using."

He ripped the bait off the hair and threw it to me. I caught it in my right hand. My eyes bulged.

"Bloody hell!" I sniffed for conformation.

"What?" Said Tony.

"Its a Streamselect Tropicano!" I said in a voice that sounded as though it didn't believe my eyes or nose for that matter.

"So?"

"Well, who'd have thought that they would be using shopboughts." I said feebly.

I didn't want to go all through my Watt-bogus bait story. Either he had fallen completely for it, had managed to go and buy some without leaving the lake and then got them to Harry or that was the THEIR bait. The Watt, Harry, Mike alliance was on, had prebaited with, were using, Tropicanos! Stranger and stranger.

"Look Matt, I've only told you about this because Dave and I consider you about the only friend we've got in this syndicate and because you let us in on Mike's hanky panky. Now keep it to yourself all right. Don't get involved, we'll level the score up with the others and then that'll be the end of it. Honours even. Ok?"

"Ok, mate. You can trust me. Now, don't get caught with that evidence will you?" I said nodding towards the three birds' nests.

Tony laughed. "No. I won't, don't worry."

I walked back to my swim brain in overdrive. I would have liked to have told Tony that the dirty trio had also been prebaiting and that to get 'honours even' he and Dave still owed Harry one and the other two, two. Of course if I told him that then they would owe me and Rambo one for prebaiting. Watt owed Mike a biggie for bonking his wife. Dave owed Kipper for pushing him off the Island. Rambo and myself were also owed by everyone for fiddling his not a twenty, twenty. I owed Watt for him lying to me about being on a sweet fishmeal bait and he owed me for telling porkies about the Tropicano. All in all it was getting difficult to remember and work out who had done what to who and how many times, even if you could cancel out debts like they taught you in primary school maths. It was only June 19th, fourth day into the season and it was all getting into a bit of a mess.

As a hindsight observation I think that after Harry's incident there was a marked change in attitude from everyone, albeit slight. People seemed to be on edge, the element of mistrust had wormed its way into the consciousness of the syndicate as a whole. Those without the 'knowledge' probably did think that kids were to blame but there was still the small nugget of doubt that gnawed away at them even though they kept it private. From that time on, all the small anxieties coupled with the extra pressure exerted by Watt's competition and the fact that all our actions could be revealed to the anecdote hungry carp magazine consuming masses meant that cards were held ever closer to chests.

Apart from Rambo being a total loner and the aloofness of the unholy trinity of Watt, Harry and Mike it had been an easy going syndicate. To be fair to those three they had on occasions helped others but not on level terms, you were still made to feel that you should be thankful but nevertheless, help it was. People had left tackle unguarded, were fairly free and easy with information and if someone was desperate to fish a certain swim they could quite often negotiate it in the car park or muck in and share a swim. That era you could call in a biblical manner, Before Harry's Incident, or BHI. After Harry's Incident (AHI) marked a subtle swing away from the desirable, of course its roots went deeper than that one action and took hold from the very beginning of my sorry tale. It was just that it was the first action that was there for all to see and consequently hit the hardest. The other, much nastier, actions were still chickens strutting around waiting to come home to roost. Anyway back to chronological time.

On the fishing front things were turning out to be as grim as we had predicted. The day passed with no action to either myself or Rambo but the others started to get the odd fish. Tony broke his duck with a nice double. Harry with new rigs and line was getting takes fairly regularly. Tradders caught, even Kipper caught and of course Watt caught and every fish he took in that session was on the rod that he had successfully negotiated into Kipper's swim. Kipper letting Watt fish his swim was perhaps the last generous, no, last over generous deed that I can remember which wasn't done due to some underhand alliance. Tencher continued to do well with the tench but his sport was starting to slow down slightly. Early evening I picked up a mirror that just made double figures from my right hand rod that I had cast as far out of the bay as I dare. I let Rambo know on the radio and he said that if I had no objections he would move down into the Oak in the morning. I told him to carry on and he then said that he would try and do a Watt and ask Tencher if he could put one bait on the Little Pads. Over and out.

Before nightfall several bivvies were moved so that they were right on top of rods, people were anxious that misfortune would not happen to them. A few, including Kipper went to the trouble of making monofilament trip wires to catch out night prowlers. At least the fool wasn't blind to the fact that he was the most vulnerable being asleep 80% of the time. Dave and Tony, I thought, overplayed the concerned syndicate member by enthusiastically making trip wires with Harry of all people. Then again they may have simply been finding out where they were so that when they slipped into action again they wouldn't end up face down in mud, fooled by the invisible properties of 12lb Maxima. Their duplicity was easy to spot especially as I had been told about it! Rambo had been on the radio and asked me what I thought about the likelihood of Harry's sabotage being kids. I felt in an awkward situation, I didn't want to go back on my word to Tony but then again I didn't want to lie to Rambo who at the end of the day, to use a football cliché, was in my team. My captain really. I sort of hinted by saying that I doubted if kids had done it and then thankfully he had sussed out the lay of the land without me saying any more, which made it much better for me. Once he had guessed I told him that the pair of them were far from finished and still reckoned on paying Tom and Mike back. He was greatly amused and expressed his glee at the impending doom that waited for Watt.

"Maybe I ought to let them buy a couple of my second hand hand grenades so that they can do a proper job," he laughed.

I laughed as well but wondered if many a true word was said in jest. The loathing that Rambo now possessed for Watt was very strong. Watt had taken the rise and would have to take the consequences. I was sure of that.

Dawn came and the night had gone. No more nasties had reared their ugly heads. Harry's throat hadn't been slit in the night and Kipper hadn't awoken to find all his gear stolen, bivvy, groundsheet the lot whipped from under his nose while he had slept on a bedchair that had been propped up on four house bricks. Bit of a shame really it would have been a photo to treasure, him still blissfully ignorant and asleep doing the human plus bedchair impression of the inner city parked, mobility challenged, wheel plundered, vandalised Ford Mondeo.

After some grub Rambo moved. I watched him cart his mass of tackle down to the Oak and having set up he went down to have a word in Tencher's ear. He came back with a flea in his own, Tencher had said no. In a way I admired him for not wilting in front of Rambo's physical intimidation and although I heard the story from both sides, eventually he had actually been quite aggressive towards Rambo. It was his swim and he was going to fish it. Rambo hadn't let Watt fish into his swim so why the bloody hell should he let Rambo do something that Rambo wasn't prepared to put up with when the boot was on the other foot. He also told Rambo that this was the first time in all the years that they had both fished the syndicate that he had ever come up to him to have a chat and all because he wanted a favour. Another dollop of inter-person stressed relations leading to group tension or whatever your local social councillor would call it and definitely symbolic of the AHI mentality.

June 20th saw the water settle down to its normal fishing pattern i.e. Watt and Harry catching well and the rest of us struggling. I was still sure of our bait but I was now in the wrong area. Rambo's results in the Oak would be a better yardstick even though he too was still at the wrong end of the lake. Watt had an early morning twenty from off the Island (good old Kipper the sycophantic lackey) and Harry caught his second at one in the afternoon, again right tight off the Big Pads. Watt and Harry were now four and two while Rambo and I were two and two in the TWTT stakes.

This was my fifth day on the water and it was a Friday, I had tomorrow and part of Sunday to fish before I had to pack up and get ready for work on the Monday. Rambo still had another week to go. What the others plans were I didn't know. I couldn't see many packing up before the weekend and guessed that quite a few would be doing much the same as myself. I now realised that this initial sprint over the first few weeks, once over, would lead to other tactics coming into consideration.

Time and effort devoted to the TWTT was going to be down to individual preferences, snatched sessions between work, whether overnighters or short before and after work ones and the commitment to full time employment as opposed to full time fishing. Then there were those guys who had shift work and could fish contrasting days and times to the rest of us. It would be quite different from the initial all there together, fishing all the time syndrome that was happening at the moment. Everything had been full tilt and we were all under each others microscope. Every move, every cast, every capture, every mishap had been seen by all, apart from Kipper who had studied the inside of his eyelids instead. If it had not been seen, then it was almost certainly heard about within hours, sometimes minutes. From now on things would be more sporadic, information and results might take days to hear about, the syndicate itself only met every two months. In the past I might not have a seen a particular member for months for one reason or another. When summer had gone and autumn and definitely when winter came it would be even worse.

I can remember thinking about all this as I sat and watched superglued indicators on that Friday afternoon. There would be occasions when certain teams might be on the water all by themselves. There would be other times when say just two opposing teams would have to carve up the water between them, again and perhaps more dangerously there would be times when single individuals from different tribes would be all alone. What would happen if Rambo and Watt were the only two soles slugging it out on a freezing afternoon in January? Would Rambo simply kill him and bury him in a shallow grave or would Watt have prudently armed himself with an AK 47 and shoot Rambo through the head in a case of pre-meditated self defence? Whatever, but I knew that the way things were starting to go with the not inconsiderable restraint of ten pairs of judicious eyes it could only deteriorate when that was no longer the case. Funnily enough the expression that is another of life's tired clichès that I was thinking of mysteriously turned up on the Saturday morning.

My mental ramblings brought on by lack of action, no fish signs and no chance to move had finished with me reciting that clichè to myself as an overall summing up of how I perceived things going when there was less of us around to check up on each others actions. I was seeing it with my own eyes some 12 hours later.

I woke up at about 6 am on Saturday after an uninterrupted night and decided to wind in for an hour and go walk-about around the lake. I had gone past the vacant Bay East swim that Rambo had left, passed the Oak and the man himself, passed Tencher and had come to Ya Man, Watt. He was staring rather quizzically at a scrap of paper that had been stuck to the back of his bivvy.

He handed it to me. "What do you make of that then, Matt?"

Totally amazed I read a scrap of paper that had the clichè, my clichè, made up from newspaper letters like a ransom note. It read: When the cat's away the mice will play. Dave and Tony were starting to slip the stiletto of Watt's unfaithful wife very slowly and carefully between his shoulder blades.

"God knows. Must be those bloody kids again," I said in best lie mode.

I made my excuses and left a bewildered Watt as quick as I could. What with this and the Tropicano bait thing I was getting punch drunk on coincidences. I nipped into a remote bush and nearly wet myself laughing, well, you laugh at anything when you're drunk and that was a something, which is much funnier.

Chapter 8

I picked up my right hand rod and did my mental space-shuttle countdown, only from twenty to give myself a fleetingly bigger chance....... -5-4-3-2-1-0, wait a fraction, no blast off and only then wind in. This was my packing up ritual as I wound in each rod, I can't remember exactly how it all started but it was no doubt caused by some last second run that had come my way and from then on I had always given it that extra-extra chance to happen again. Despite having three bites at the cherry nothing materialised and soon three rods were halved and in the ubiquitous Nash holdall. By then, naturally, everything else had been stored as the rods were always the last to get put away. A whole weeks fishing, night and day was over for another year but unlike other years a fire still burned in my belly.

After such a long session, for me anyway, I was normally happy to call it a day and have a break from fishing for a while, but not this time. The TWTT was up for grabs and I had a personal vendetta list as long as a match fisherman's pole. The week had ended with myself and Rambo trailing behind Harry and Tom in the twenty captures department, the opposition had three and four while I had two and Rambo now had three. He had taken his third twenty that very Sunday morning when I was thinking that I had only eight or so hours to go before my real life came barging into this session and dragged me by the scruff of the neck back to reality, bills, relationships and that most disgusting of ogres, work.

Fishing from the Oak with Cold War style hostilities very much in the air with Tencher in the Little Pads, Rambo had struck metaphoric gold in the shape of a super common that had weighed in at just over 21lb. Our bait was still a good one. The last two days or so had been disappointing for me personally after a cracking start. Unable to move from the Bay West swim unlike the carp, there was little I could do at the time to get back on the fish. I vowed to come back as soon as I could in the evenings and get into one of the more productive swims. My last chore, therefore, before I left the lake was to find out when the others were going to pack in and find out what was likely to be available.

I popped back to the 1st Twenty to see Tradders, he was off in a few hours and had seen Tony in the Pines who along with side-kick Dave were also going sometime today. Harry was staying another week which was bad news, I couldn't see him moving out from such a good swim and he was bound to catch. I wished Tradders all the best and went back to my swim. Loaded to the gunwales with tackle I staggered round to Rambo to wish him luck. I told him what the others were up to and I said that I would try and find what Tom was doing and let him know via the radio. Rambo told me that it was powerful enough for me to reach him from my home or vice versa which would be well handy. I told him that I would take it to work so that he could tell me if anything important had happened or if a good swim became available. He gave me the thumbs up and I left him, a few words with Tencher and I struggled on to the junction of the path between the Wide and the Island that lead to the car park. Kipper was flat out on his bedchair but Watt was very much awake. I put down my gear and went over to see the old git.

"Worked out what that note was all about then, Tom," I asked mischievously. It was great knowing. I'd seen more of Watt's wife in the last week than he had but not as much as Mike had seen, or fondled or fornicated.

"No, I haven't. I don't think it really means anything, it's just some small-minded individual trying to divert my attention away from my fishing. Which they've failed," added Tom haughtily.

"So you think it's one of us then?" I asked, stirring the pot.

"Probably."

"Yet you think that it was kids who cut Harry's sounder box cables?"

"Yes. That type of wanton vandalism typifies today's society, particularly the younger generation. None of us would do that type of thing but this note nonsense is a different kettle of fish altogether. Equally pathetic in its own way but the work of someone trying to play little psychological mind games and definitely not a child. Well not in a physical sense, maybe a mental one." Watt smiled at his own adroitness with words and then continued. "I have a pretty shrewd idea who the perpetrator is in any case."

"Really!" I said in high excitement calculated to pump Watt's ego even larger. "Who! For God's sake!"

"Rambo!" He said smugly.

"Rambo!?" Not even close mate, but interesting.

"Yes. I think that when I caught the two twenties when you had left the water for an hour..."

"Two hours." I corrected him before Watt could make his achievements sound even grander.

"Whatever, I think that when I cajoled him after the captures about him helping me by not letting me fish where I wanted to, an outrageous action, it really got to the sad boy. Underneath all that macho exterior for all his physical prowess there lurks a very weak individual."

I could have taken exception to so much that Watt was rattling on about but it would have to wait. "How much longer are you fishing for, then?" I said changing the subject.

"Kipper is here until Tuesday, then I'll probably move into the Island and fish it for the rest of next week. Harry and I originally planned to have two weeks on the water."

I remember thinking that Mike was going to end up with a sore dick and have an expensive Vaseline bill considering some of the sexual deviations himself and Jennifer preferred. She might rather stand than sit.

I nodded to Watt. "Well, don't catch too many and watch out Rambo doesn't send you a letter bomb rather than just a note. I'll see you later."

With that I went and got my gear and carted it all back up to the car park and my waiting van. Despite it being much lighter than when I came a week ago it was hard work due to lack of motivation. I was not looking forward to the building site on Monday, I wanted to be at the lake with Rambo slugging it out toe to toe with Harry and Watt. Another week and they might have caught so much that my challenge would be effectively over by the second week of the season. I would just have to make the effort to get there as much as I could. Sophie wouldn't like it, that was certain, but I'd have to cross that bridge later.

I had finally got everything into the back of my van when Dave and Tony lurched into the car park. I went to see them. They had changed, it was hard to explain but these two boys weren't the two shy Noddies from a week ago. Getting the shitty end of the stick and catching a few fish had galvanised them into a pair of blokes quite capable of sticking up for themselves. As if to underline their new found authority the pair of them let down all four of Watt's car tyres and in a moment of madness brought on by the stimulation of hissing air Dave put a boulder through Kipper's 'D' reg Cavalier's front offside headlight. The sound of breaking glass brought instant sobriety, I was as shocked as the headlight. Dave was turning a bit pale, he licked his lips and looked for support from me and Tony. I gave it.

"Don't worry, he won't bloody hear it. He'll still be asleep."

We all laughed and we all got out the car park as quick as we could like scampering schoolboys who had knocked on some mean old sod's front door. Driving off at boy racer pace I hoped that neither Watt or Kipper came to their vehicles for a long time, at least then there was a chance of blaming someone else. It would have been difficult to say that the damage had already been done now that we had left as any descent person would have gone back and reported the damage. Still the syndicate was fast running out of descent people, Tradders, Kipper and even Tencher were the only three that could be cleared of malicious intent and cheating. Kipper's row with Dave over the Island swim hardly deserved a vandalised car and having got the swim the old fool had handed the best bit of it on a plate to Watt.

Work came hard on Monday. I made a couple of stupid mistakes all because my mind was elsewhere, the elsewhere being the syndicate lake of course where I was determined to fish that evening. As luck would have it my boss left early and I left just after him! I hammered it down the road so fast that it crossed my mind that if I didn't back off a bit I might end up overtaking him. By four I was in the car park frantically getting my gear out when the farmer who's land our lake was on wandered up to me and said hello. I was so intent on getting my gear out that I had neither heard or seen him approach me. His sudden appearance on my shoulder made me jump.

"Christ! You nearly gave me a heart attack. I didn't hear you." I said genuinely startled.

"No, you didn't old young' un. Mind you I 'eard them there police sirens this mornin', rushin' up here they was, 'cos of them there cars that had been damaged." Said the farmer.

"Oh," I said, "what was all that about then?"

The old boy transfixed me with his keen eyes that burnt out of his ruddy face. I hoped he couldn't tell what a complete liar I was. Despite his rural vernacular that gave the impression of a country dullard I knew him to be a shrewd old stick and not backward in coming forward when it came to money. He was as shabby as a vagrant but his farmhouse was beautiful and had at least three BMWs parked outside it.

"Well old Tom Watt phoned 'em after he found 'is car had been tampered with. Old Kipper's was as well. So, the Old Bill came up 'ere makin' a tidy old racket and Watt reported it." Suddenly the farmer grabbed my arm in a tight powerful grip. Shocked I looked down at his brown, gnarled hand that threatened to cut off the circulation to my left hand. "D' you know what 'e 'ad the bloody cheek to say? Eh?"

This obviously required an answer from me so I said. "No," as positively as I could. He released my arm.

"Well, 'e said that it was probably my grandchildren. Yes! The bloody cheek of 'im, my grandchildren.'E also said that they had been a causin' other trouble, muckin' around with some of your fishin' tackle an' all that. Old 'igh an' mighty Tom Watt a sayin' what 'e likes whether it were true or not. Them's coppers came round to my place asking where my grandchildren were at such and such a time and that they had reason to believe that they were a causin' trouble all because that big'ead 'ad said so."

I was impressed that the farmer had Tom weighed up so spot on and that Tom had so spectacularly upset him. I had met the old boy a few times before and had treated him with the utmost respect. You tend to be like that when somebody owns something that you treasure and especially when he is letting you use it or rather lease it. He had struck me as a deep character, I thought the veneer of his roughness and lack of articulation cloaked an astute and crafty schemer. He had the common touch but his word was probably good enough to trust your mortgage on. He carried on talking.

"You know I've always 'ad me doubts about that there Tom Watt. Too wordy by 'alf..." The old boy's eyes seemed to twinkle as again he gazed deep into my own, "it 'ardly seems worth all that effort of puttin' up with seein' 'im too often......all for fourteen 'undred pounds or so a year...." He let his words sink into my brain as I frantically tried to turn it into some kind of mathematical calculator.

"The lease for this year is fourteen hundred pounds?" I said shocked.

"Give or take a few shillings," smiled the farmer. "Somethin' a troublin' you old young' un?"

"We all paid two hundred and twenty-five quid this year. Ten of us paid two hundred and twenty-five pounds!"

"Well, there you are, think on then. Looks like the two cars that got the damage were the right' uns."

And with that he went! I couldn't believe it, I was absolutely blown away! For five minutes I just stood and gaped and thought and gaped and stood and stared and wondered and then gaped again for good measure.

The implications were without any ambiguity, the farmer niggled by Watt to such an extent had decided to casually drop into the conversation a few confidential financial details. He had clearly thought that there might have been a few fiddles going on which I had confirmed to him with my reaction. My reading of the situation was that he had been happy enough with what he was getting, he hardly needed to grind us into the ground for an extra few hundred and had not concerned himself with our internal affairs and fiscal policy. That had now changed because Watt had upset him and he had decided to finger him and Kipper, his last remark about the cars could only mean that the pair of them were ripping us off. Even if you allowed a couple of hundred notes which would be ample for any expenses, the pair of them were making about three hundred a year each out of the rest of us. Nice bit of tackle box money for our two co-founders. No wonder Kipper let Watt fish off the Island, he was paying him back for Watt cutting him in on the scam.

We had always paid our money direct to Watt in cash because we had been told that the farmer didn't want to have it go through the books and therefore avoid the double whammy of the Inland Revenue and VAT, which supposedly saved us money as well. Talk about lambs to the slaughter. Although Watt did have the lease tied up for as long as we came up with the readies and at an inflation linked rate it also meant that we were being overcharged at an inflation linked rate. Between us we had put about fifteen hundred quid snugly into Watt and Kipper's back pockets over the six years we had been going. What a syndicate it was turning out to be! Peace and harmony for six years and then POW!

I grabbed my gear and headed down to the lake, as I walked down the path I resolved to keep this new info under my hat and not to tell anyone, even Rambo, until I had thought it through properly.

That evening I fished like a man possessed, for once I read the water correctly and it paid dividends. Harry was still in the Big Pads, Watt the Wide, Kipper the Island and Rambo had moved into the Little Pads because Tencher had left or Rambo had murdered him and shoved him in some shallow grave somewhere along with his tackle, with a tin of sweetcorn as the headstone. The rest of the swims were free and while having a look at them I spotted a fish roll in the Deep corner and decided to fish there. I set up quickly and soon had three rods out, two in the area where I had seen the fish roll straight out from the bank some twenty yards. I put out about fifty baits in a six foot circle around them and waited. I had spoken to no-one and I didn't feel like getting on the radio to Rambo either, to be honest I was sick of the lot of them.

An hour later the middle rod ripped off, I was on it quickly and lent into what appeared to feel like a good fish. I had been playing it for no more than ten seconds when the right rod, which had been in the same area, went as well. Confident that it had been well hooked by my 3oz bolt rig I left it to tear off and hoped that it wouldn't snag up or if it did I could pull out of it. My only concession was to turn off the alarm, there was no way I could play a fish in with a 100 decibel Optonic pulsing in my ear. I decided to go for it and bullied the first fish as much as I dared.

Luck was with me and I landed it fairly quickly, some of the side strain that I used when the fish was in close was way above my normal level of doing things, for once I didn't back-wind. As soon as the first fish was unhooked and put in a sack which unusually I did with minimum fuss and maximum dexterity, I hit the second. I wound down quickly to find that the fish had run off to the left tip of the Island and had sulked under some overhanging branches, just then the third rod........ only joking boys, this is the real world I'm talking about but then perhaps for some of you I'm out of it already. Anyway, to cut a dogged fight short I pumped the fish off of the Island and got it back out in front of me. Then of course I played it out in my normal (some would say over-fussy) way, back-winding at every surge but nevertheless successfully. The second fish was much the better, (23lb 6ozs) and the first was still a very nice double (15lb 10ozs).

I took the first fish out of the sack and put her into my weigh sling and the second one went straight into the sack after unhooking. The reason for all the jiggery pokery was because I would have to get one of the others to witness what I was certain was a twenty, whereas I was happy to pop the fifteen straight back after I had weighed it. I had just got the second fish into the water all nicely tucked up in a sack and was about to weigh the first when Harry arrived on the scene. For the second time that evening I had been engrossed and had failed to notice the fact that I had company.

"Need any help?" he asked.

"Only to do a few photographs of the fish and witness what I'm sure is a twenty. If you don't mind that is," I replied cordially.

"If you think that's a twenty you better have your eyes and scales tested," said Harry contemptuously while looking at the first fish in the sling.

He was blissfully unaware of my double capture and the singular and plural of fish being equivocal. He'd probably been having a piddle when it all happened, he always seemed to be.

"Not that one you prick. The one in the sack's a twenty. That one's a mid double," I retorted offensively. It went quiet. I wondered if he would let it ride and how accurate I could guess fish weights.

"Give me your camera then," he said coldly.

The pair of us went through the motions of photographing and weighing the two fish in virtual silence. Harry got his own back by making the fish 23lb 5 instead of the 23lb 6, I reckoned it was just to try and assert a little fishing seniority. I let him get on with it the silly bastard. I'd caught them and it had bugged him. A dork like me catching with runs at the same time should never happen, it was written all over his face. I tried to make my face seem like it had the middle digit stuck up straight written all over it. I'm not a confrontational person or wasn't until all the pus had started to ooze out the syndicate, but that evening I felt really obnoxious to all of them. Watt came down while I was holding the twenty to poke his nose in and noticed a severe lack of Tropicano on my rigs. My true bait was there for all to see, it was too bad. I put the fish back, Watt entered it into the Twenty Log book and Harry pushed off but Watt lingered.

"Well, two at once, very impressive," said Watt, "and on a new bait by the looks of it. Rather a brave move to change baits after you've been doing so well on your other one. It looks a very similar bait to the one Rambo's using, certainly the same colour. Still it works."

"It sure does" I said, my temper beginning rise, not so much by what Tom was saying but because of the situation his words were putting me in.

He knew I had lied about the Tropicano, he had probably watched me cast with binoculars and knew I was lying from the start. I suddenly felt like a boy carper in the presence of a pro. Then I remembered that he had told me he was on a sweet fish-meal but if I wanted to bring that up I had to box clever. If I told him that he had lied about his bait I would have to explain that, A) I had found out he was on Tropicanos by virtue of what Harry was on when his rigs had been pulled in and also B) that to know they were both on the same bait it would have to be because I had heard them prebaiting when I had been prebaiting my own. All very complicated.

" I guess it's no business of yours what bait I'm on. Have you ever told me what you're using?" I said trying to muster up some defence.

"I told you exactly what bait I was on, a sweetened fishmeal with Mega tutti-frutti," said Watt matching my sarcasm.

"So you say," I replied.

"Are you calling me a liar then," said Watt indignantly.

"Maybe you've been lying about a whole load of things," I said warming to my task. "Maybe you're not the type of person you like to make out you are. If we're talking about lying then maybe I know more than you can ever dream of. You might think that you can present this holier-than- thou image but it's slipped and behind it it's like a pint of maggots crawling all over the Sunday joint."

Both our minds boggled as we tried to get to grips with my rather shaky imagery but I could tell Watt was not so self assured. "What do you mean? What are you on about?"

I looked at him just like the farmer had eyeballed me. I knew I lacked his grizzled countenance but what the hell. "I know all about it." I said deliberately. Enigma, what a weapon.

"All about what?" Said Watt trying to front me out.

"All about your dirty little dealings. I'd take the time to tell you but I've got to get back for work tomorrow morning." Sarcasm as well. I was on a roll.

"It was you who damaged my car and Kipper's wasn't it?" said Watt, counter-attacking. "I've noticed an attitude change in you lately, you've got some ridiculous notion that I've wronged you and now you're trying..."

The words froze in Watt's mouth as my third rod, the only one left on my rack happily rattled away to the Optonic concerto for Super XL in 'D' minor, fortissimo. With a nonchalant 'How' Indian hand greeting to Watt that said 'step back, sonny', I strutted to my rod and played in a beautiful fully-scaled mirror that turned out to be a thumping 24lb exactly. I can tell you that after such a cocky approach even though I'm an atheist I was praying to God that I could land the fish and it wouldn't come off. It would have been a shrivel up and die job otherwise, anyway, someone answered my prayers, it was probably those two Sunday school visits and a church wedding that done it. I believe! I believe! Well I did for a few minutes. Funny, you don't accept God and then as soon as the shit hits the fan its 'please God this' and 'please God that'. No wonder He gets fed up with us and kills a few of us off! I held the scales up so that Watt could verify the weight, he barely looked and nodded his acknowledgement grudgingly.

"Stick that in your log book and smoke it," I said, to effectively end our discussion. As Watt walked back to his swim he told me to 'fuck off.' I had never heard him swear before and felt pleased that I had got to him enough to make him do it. I fished on in a dream wondering whether in fact I was in one. It was a wet one that was for sure. By ten, (no more action) I had to go, I hadn't eaten and Sophie would be getting the hump. I told Rambo all about it on the radio and was pleased to hear that he had caught a couple of nice fish since getting into the Little Pads. I packed up sharpish and went home, needless to say Watt never said good-bye.

I was keen to tell Sophie what I had caught and rushed indoors. She was not keen to listen, apparently my boss had come back having forgotten something and was less than ecstatic that I had cleared off. He had phoned up earlier on in the evening to find out why I wasn't on site when I should have been. Sophie had had the brains to tell him that I had a dentist's appointment but was less than happy about having to do it. I got the, you-need-this-job-to-pay-the-mortgage-you've-just-had-a-whole-week-fishing-what-about-me-stuck-on-my-own, speech, which no doubt you've all heard in some fashion or another. It was fair comment, I was being selfish and decided to agree with her.

Later that evening when I hoped that she would be more receptive I asked if she minded if I went tomorrow evening. She went up the wall and grounded me until Saturday with a list of things we were to do together the following evenings. Being a wimp I let it ride, besides I could toy with my new exposure about Watt the embezzler and how to use it to my advantage and there were some boilies to be made as well. A few days away from fishing would also give me time to consider the overall picture of the syndicate, the politics and scores to be settled by members who had been wronged or cheated by other members. It was becoming more tangled than a two foot multistrand confidence rig without tubing, gel or PVA. Two months ago it had been harmony and light and friendly work parties, but then no-one had known what everyone else was up to. With revelation after revelation piling up the S.S had achieved the impossible, we made politicians look respectable. No mean feat.

Chapter 9

My week of abstinence from the TWTT hunt passed grudgingly. One night spent at Tesco, a real riot that was barging through all the long lost friend conversations taking part slap bang in the middle of the aisles, one night goggle-box gawping and one night boilie making. Actually the boilie making night was my most reserved, one drop of mix on the floor and my guts would have been the proverbial garters. When I think how I had mixed bait at Rambo's compared to how I did it at home it was the sublime (in terms of quantity and speed) to the ridiculous. Why at home I even washed my hands before I turned the tap on so that the handle didn't get cacked up! (Come on, think about it.) I was orderly, organised and tidy and about ten times slower but eventually I got there. I also ordered some more base mix and flavouring from .... no way! Thursday night I tried to get hold of Rambo on the radio but with no success. The radio was virtually like a CB unit and although I stuck to the right frequency I couldn't get hold of him. For two hours I played at aural voyeurism listening in on all the rubbish that people come out with when afforded the ace card of anonymity. It was sad, almost as sad as listening to it I guess!

On the Friday night I was hoping to get to the lake at about five straight from work and miss the early hours of Saturday rush but Sophie had other ideas and insisted that I took her out for a meal. Sneakily I booked the table as early as I could saying it was the only time available, the logic being that the quicker I could get the meal over the quicker I could skedaddle down to the lake and get a better swim. This all backfired on me when the pair of us got to the restaurant at seven p.m. and ate alone until nine when some more punters eventually turned up. Sophie had gotten irate, she had been less than happy about eating so early and had unfortunately sussed my tactical ploy early on.

"You only booked this early so that you could get to fishing quicker, didn't you?" She said as the main course arrived. "Look! They're not exactly stacked out with customers are they?" She continued while the waitress put our food down. I knew she was annoyed because normally our conversations tended to dry up when the food is served.

"Maybe they had a load of last minute cancellations," I said, waiting for the waitress to be out of earshot..

"For Christ sake, Matt! Don't insult my intelligence, please. I know perfectly why you booked early, and don't think that I'm not going to have a sweet and coffee as well. We've come out for a meal and we're going to eat one in a relaxed manner ......"

"You don't seem very relaxed," I interrupted.

She was not side-tracked. ".....In a relaxed manner, not worrying about how fast you can get the food down your neck so that you can go bloody fishing. I'm getting fed up with it, you seem obsessed with it. Prior to this year you've always been sensible about it. You used to tell me how the others let fishing dictate their lives to the detriment of everything else, their jobs, their families, their responsibilities. You used to say how daft they were and now you're turning into one of them."

I know, I thought but it's different this year. So much is different and you just don't understand how it has got to me. "I'm sorry," I said, "anyway I thought you liked me fishing and enjoying myself, it's the one hobby I've got." I said trying the old sympathy crack.

"Don't be ridiculous. There's a difference between scratching your arse and tearing the skin off."

"Well maybe you could become involved more rather than sitting at home waiting for me. I mean you enjoyed it when you took me and Rambo to the lake that evening," I said.

"If you think I'm going to spend days sitting watching you fishing you've got another think coming."

"You could help me make my boilies." I said with genuine enthusiasm that was rapidly crushed.

"Oh thanks! Very generous of you. If you were as keen to cook the evening meal as you were to make those boilies I might think about helping but you're normally slumped in front of the telly while I'm slaving over the stove."

"Slaving over the microwave buttons with a T.V dinner more like," I said sarcastically, "I'm surprised you haven't picked up a repetitive injury strain on your index finger or at least a blister."

"There's no chance of you picking up any strain with what you've been doing at home," she retaliated with a note of finality.

That brief exchange that had 'married couple' written all over it set the tone for the rest of the evening. She was annoyed and to be frank I was more interested in getting to the lake than worrying about it. What a dork I was to treat her like that especially after all that was to happen later when she would become the one thing I could hang onto...... and that she let me, despite it all she let me. Anyway at the time I never really realised how selfish I had become.

After what seemed to be about four years I eventually got home and changed and slung all my gear in the van. I told Sophie that I'd be back for Sunday afternoon and I did love her. She managed to smile and kissed me good-bye and hoped that I caught something. Off I shot, the time now 11: 30pm, it was to be a set up in the dark job and I was hoping that the weather kept fair so that I could forget about having to put up a bivvy by torch light. Although, like I mentioned, I wasn't a great fan of night fishing, it now seemed to be a necessity to optimise all my time and get in before rest of the weekenders bowled up. I drove like a lunatic to the lake and had to really slam on the anchors to avoid a badger which decided to wander out in front of me. At last I got to the car park and my spirits sunk.

I was deflated by the dreaded full-car-park scenario, that most frustrating of situations that I know all of you have encountered. More cars means less room and less room means less choice and in all likelihood poorer choice which ultimately can lead to less fish. This happenstance is all the more gauling when you have busted a gut to get there as early as possible usually after upsetting some loved one in the process or having run the risk of getting the sack. When you have arrived at what you would consider to be an early enough time to secure at least a good choice of swims it is even worse. Everybody else had thought the same but had been able to make it before me, a check amongst the cars indicated a full house, even Mike had turned up, the novelty of Watt's wife no doubt fading.

As I walked to the lake I wondered where I would end up fishing, probably in a puddle on the path. I went through the swims in my mind mentally ticking each one off in order of likely occupancy. I reckoned I would end up in the bay somewhere, a thought that hardly gripped me with excitement. If the fish had moved back up there then you could bet that both the bay swims would be gone, if they hadn't then one would be vacant. Great! I decided to ask Rambo who was where because I certainly didn't want to lug all my gear around the lake looking for the one empty swim.

When I got to the Little Pads I downed tackle and went to his bivvy. Rambo was awake and was cutting the cuticles off his fingernails with a huge bowie-knife by torch light. One slip and he would have had his arm off. He was pleased to see me and filled me in on who had done what and more importantly who had caught what and where they were fishing. It made uncomfortable listening, both Watt and Harry resident in the two best swims had caught steadily all week. Watt now had seven twenties to his name, Harry five, Rambo now had four like myself and two new names had been added to the log. Both Dave and Tony had caught their first ever respective twenties on Wednesday evening while they had shared the Pines swim. I was chuffed for them partly because I didn't consider them a viable threat for the trophy. I was less happy about Watt and Harry forging ahead but there was little I could do about it other than try and catch more.

As I had expected all the swims were gone except for the Bay West, my opening day swim. Rambo was sure that nothing much was happening up there and kindly said I could share the Little Pads with him. I didn't need asking twice even though it meant that our alliance would be revealed to a certain extent. Eagerly I set up and cast out to the right hand set of pads as best I could in the dark. Rambo had two baits out on the left hand set and one in-between and now my three were out there as well. One good sideways belting run from one of the end rods and it could be crochet time. I'd worry about that when it happens I told myself. Which it didn't.

Dawn broke after a runless night in which I had spent a good deal of gassing with Rambo. The major topic was when Watt and Harry would leave the water, their initial two week stint finished Sunday and the pair of us wondered if there would be a wildebeest-like stampede to occupy either the Big Pads or the Island. Who would constitute the herd was the other question. Rambo said that he could stay on for another week seeing as he didn't have to rush off to some exotic climate and machine gun somebody. I wished I could join him but good old work loomed over my head like a rabid vulture waiting to peck my eyes out if I did. The vulture's name was Sophie Responsibility Billpayer.

Of the others it seemed unlikely that any of them would be around during the day as all of them worked and had already taken time off for the first week. It seemed as if Rambo had a good chance to catch up if not overtake the field. He could be a one man marauding herd of swim-savvy wildebeest. Rambo had also said that any evening I came along I could share one of the good swims with him provided I brought him some more food and boilies. It seemed well fair to me. Let them know we were a pair, it didn't really matter now and it certainly didn't matter to me if I could cash in on the best swims and Rambo was happy enough to let me. In any case Watt had noticed that we were on a similar boilie and was clever enough to put two and two together and come up with four.

As Saturday morning passed with little action to anyone I wondered if Dave and Tony were going to cough up some nasty little surprise for Mike. He was the last person to be paid back, Watt, Kipper and Harry had all been done over and if the pair of them were true to their word that would be the end of it. Of course they didn't have the extra knowledge that I had, the biggy about Watt and Kipper stitching all of us up on the syndicate money front but they did know about Mike and Watt's wife. Would there be more paste up notes to work Watt's brain into a stew. If there was, Rambo would get the blame because Watt had decided that he had done it. It certainly added another dimension to the fishing, more stress as well.

As I looked around the lake on that June morning with Rambo's super binoculars I took note of all the bivvies perched on top of three rod set ups. The AHI (after Harry incident) mentality was very much alive and kicking, even Dave and Tony had pitched their respective bivvies likewise even though they were the ones who had caused the incident. They didn't want to draw any comments obviously, only Rambo had bucked the trend but then maybe he had mined the area around his rods and only he himself knew the safe route. Mind you, I know I'd still end up in smithereens if I'd done that, as soon as that alarm screams the brain goes totally one track.

I noticed that Mike was fishing the Deep Corner (the swim where I had taken my two twenties on Monday evening) which rested between the Big Pads and the Island where Harry and Watt were. The big three all in a line, and two of them on no-speaking terms with yours truly, I had yet to upset Mike but easily could especially if I told Watt a little story. Dave was in the swim next to us, the Wide, and I felt compelled to quickly pop and ask him if Mike was in for any shocks, so I nipped down to him to have a quick chat. Just as I got to him his middle rod powered off with a mega-belter and he was soon into playing a powerful fish. Feeling kindly disposed to the bloke I got his landing net and asked if he wanted me to net the fish for him which he did. I waited patiently as he played the fish which swam deep and hard around ten yards out, reluctant to show fin or scale of itself. The water boiled a lot and despite as much pressure as he dared try Dave couldn't get the fish up to the surface which I always reckon to be the sign of a pretty hefty beast. Five more minutes passed and eventually Dave's rig tube broke the surface and soon after we both got a good look at what appeared to be a large mirror.

"Looks like one for Tom's Log Book," I said.

"Yeah," said Dave in a voice heavily laced with tension. I knew how he felt.

By now I had carefully put his net in the water and was kneeling down waiting for the fish to tire and let its head come up. It seemed to have little intention of doing this by the way it was still charging up and down the margins but eventually the runs got shorter and less powerful and Dave could turn the fish much easier. I stood up still slightly stooped to do my bit for him. Dave gave a bit more welly and the fish turned on its side with its head up, easing back he dragged the fish towards the net which I moved slowly out toward the fish. Just as it got to the edge of the net the bloody thing gave one last desperate slap of its tail, shot across the corner of the net before I could lift it and the hook pulled. The bomb winged out of the water and hit Dave right in the middle of the forehead while I groped at empty water in a vain attempt at netting the already departed.

"Bollocks!" Dave shouted as he turned away clutching one hand to his smitten brow whilst jettisoning the rod with the other. He rubbed his forehead vigorously and turned his wrath on me. "Thanks a fucking bundle. Great work on the net. What the fuck were you trying to do, poke it in the eye?"

"What are you on about? I didn't do anything wrong," I said somewhat taken aback.

"From where I was standing it looked to me as if you did everything wrong," said a third voice. I looked around in total rage to see Watt standing some six or so yards behind me and Dave. Watt continued. "I saw you deliberately wriggle the net as the fish was coming in so that it was spooked. That carp was ready for netting and David here would have been weighing in another twenty if it wasn't for you. Maybe you don't like it when other people have some good fortune."

I was beside myself with fury. "Are you going to listen to all this shit," I said to Dave, "knowing what this bastard has been up to?" Apparently he was because Dave told me to butt out in no uncertain terms.

"Next time I hook a fish Williams just stay out the way. I might have a chance to land it then without you coming round and screwing everything up for me, you pillock."

I can tell you I was gobsmacked, even now all this time later I struggle to find the words to describe exactly how I felt. I did feel bad about Dave losing the fish but I swear on my mother's life that I tried to net that fish 100%. We've all lost fish at the net for some reason or another and it is a nasty experience but I'm as positive as I could be that I was just Mr Scapegoat on that occasion. Things like that happen in fishing, now I wouldn't offer to net anything for anybody unless specifically asked and even then not without a signed disclaimer form exonerating myself from any mishaps. In America they've probably got them already with precise reference to pulled hooks, snapped lines, tangles, net lunging, premature netting attempt, delayed netting attempt and such like. I bet they've got lawyers making a fortune out of lost fish litigation and compensation. As well as ambulance chasers they've got loads of lawyers just hanging around lakes and rivers all waiting for the cry, ' hey Bud, get the net I've got a big one'.

The thing about it all that really got to me was Watt's comments. I reckoned that he hadn't hardly seen anything but a good opportunity to divide and rule and make me the villain of the piece. It was just revenge for our little fracas on the Monday evening that was all. It also made it clear that he wasn't going to let it ride and was undoubtedly running me down behind my back with all the other syndicate members. If Dave was going to side with him, admittedly under a situation of duress, what about the others? They didn't know about Watt, the draw and prebaiting and so had no axe to grind and were bound to side with him. Maybe only Tradders would be unmoved by Watt's bilious rhetoric.

As I returned to my swim I felt ever more alienated. When I got there Rambo was having a brew. He offered me a mug of fresh tea, it tasted like nectar.

"Well, mate. Its you and me against the rest of the world," I said gravely.

"What's happened now?" He asked. "I heard some sort of commotion over there." I told him the latest and he received the news with a derisory snort.

"I'll tell you," I said starting to babble, "it's us against them. Watt will be winding them other tossers up like clockwork toys against me and you. You know he's got you down for the funny note on the bivvy that Dave and Tony put there and now he knows we're an item in the fishing sense he'll be double gunning for the pair of us. I'll tell you what, I reckon that if he could get us out the syndicate he would. What is it seven members against an individual on a vote to out them?" Rambo nodded. "He could get that. Me, you, maybe Tradders, who else would back us? Tencher won't after he fell out with you over where you wanted to fish. Kipper's his lap dog, then there's Harry. Mike! What a joke. Dave and Tony now because those two won't split, the pair of sad dopes and pus head himself. Seven! Goodnight Vienna!"

Rambo looked at me with a hint of a smile on his lips. "Easy, boy. Calm down and wipe the spittle from those ranting lips. Incidentally, how long have you had this paranoia?" I pulled a face at him. Rambo threw the dregs of tea from his cup and stood up with an air of authority. "In any case you have nothing to worry about on that score, believe me."

"Why's that then ?" I asked.

"Because they're shit scared of me, that's why. If they tried to ban me and you I'd be forced to take the lot of them apart limb by limb and they know that, and that is why they won't."

"Is violence your answer to every problem?" I asked him.

Rambo paused for a micro second to contemplate this. "Yeah, basically. You see at the end of the day it's all about how big your stick is and how hard you can swing it. Even with governments, when you get down to the wire after all the mouth, it's that that counts." He screwed up his fist and clenched it. Imagine five bananas wrapped around a coconut and you've got it. "Money is the second thing of course because you can buy muscle with money. Muscle and equipment to do the job."

"Muscle like you," I said. He nodded. "Well here's ten pee," I chucked a coin in front of him, "pop down to that local hardware shop and get a small thermo-nuclear device and drop it on Watt's bivvy."

"Now that, I would do for nothing," he laughed.

"While we're on the subject of money I would like to tell you a story that a little old man told to me last Monday. Supply my lips with another mug of your best beverage and I will tell you a tale of treachery and betrayal that will make your braid curl. It is another reason why we will never be thrown out of the SS."

Rambo made tea and I told him about the confab I had had with the farmer who owns the lake and how he had implied that Watt and Kipper were ripping us off. Rambo didn't need to go to a hardware shop for the nuclear device. He became one, one that had just gone off. I thought that he had got pretty upset when I had told him about the first day draw swim rigging while we were at his flat making the boilies but that had just been a mild outburst compared to the one that confronted me now. Try and envisage the best pyrotechnic explosion that big budget Hollywood has ever produced, then double it and you have a rough visual approximation of Rambo's paddy. As the last flickering embers gradually went out some ten minutes later and the air lost its deep blue colour they were replaced with a huge malevolent brooding.

Rambo sat on his lounger uncoiling 15lb Big Game Line off a bulk spool he had just taken out of his rucksack. He held the spool in his left hand whilst wrapping line around his right hand as he stared into nowhere. When the end had gone around his hand four or so times he jerked his two arms apart breaking the line with a noisy crack off. I looked for severed fingers but none existed. Unbelievably he just went on monotonously breaking off two foot lengths of line, which I guessed were a poor substitute for Watt and Kipper's scraggy necks, with effortless, painless ease.

The effect was quite frightening, he seemed totally introverted even slightly crazed and although I could predict the next crack off because of his metronomic timing (ten seconds) it still made me blink and twitch involuntarily. Much like a recently mutilated body I thought pointedly. After ten minutes of this my nerves were starting to fray and Rambo showed no inclination towards stopping and I was not going to ask him. My mind began to jangle, 15lb Big Game Line comes on a 900 yard spool, say at best 500 yards left, that's 1,500 ft, at 2ft every ten seconds. 1,500 divided by two is 750. 750 times ten is 7,500, divide that by 60 makes 125 minutes. Fucking hell, I thought, two hours of this and I'll end up insane and I started to count the snap-offs because the noise consumed my whole existence and it seemed the only thing to do.

At a merciful 182, (maybe he got bored) Rambo stopped, chucked the spool back into his rucksack and got up.

"Ok," he said as if nothing had happened, "we'll bear that in mind on future occasions," and we carried on fishing as if I had never told him.

I managed to get a quick gander at his right hand an hour or so later and it looked as if it had pulled Pavarotti out of a 100 ft hole with, well 15lb Big Game Line actually and the line hadn't snapped. His hand was a mass of deep indentations but no cuts, his skin must have been as thick as an elephants hide. Monofilament masochism, that's what I called it, Rambo probably considered it some sort of relaxation technique. By the way bird-lovers, I picked up all the odd bits of line.

The weekend hurried on, you think... wow! 40 hours carp fishing and it goes in about six. On the whole, the lake fished poorly but Rambo and I managed two fish each which I think was better than anyone else. Dave's lost fish would have been the best by a fair margin and therefore the Log Book went untroubled, the weekend was the equivalent of cricket's dot ball. Only Tradders came around to have a chat to the pair of us, he had news from the grapevine that was of interest. Apparently Watt was smarming over both Dave and Tony, offering advice and doing his gracious best to underline his new allegiance. I couldn't really believe that the pair of them could turn so quickly, it was less than a week since they had deflated Watt's tyres.

Maybe Dave really did believe I had tried, succeeded, in making him lose a good fish and that had just put everything on its head. Tradders also said that a few murmurings were afoot about who was responsible for the car damage and Watt's anonymous note. Guess who? And perhaps, with hindsight, Harry's sounder box cables. Guess who again? Basically the pair of us were getting fitted up with all the nastiness by rumourmonger Watt. We were now official whipping boys and it crossed my mind that maybe a few people were getting cold feet about all the aggro and cheating and were trying to get out of what they had done by dumping us two unpopular saps in it up to our necks. I didn't want to sour Tradders any more by telling him the whole sordid truth, he seemed upset enough as it was. He still blamed the introduction of the TWTT and I guess it did have a fair bit to do with it. He also said that he would stick up for the pair of us if anybody slagged us off as he knew we weren't that type. I was genuinely touched and felt guilty about some of the things that I had done in the name of vengeance against other people's prior misdemeanours that had affected him.

I packed up at about six that Sunday afternoon. I call six the afternoon because that was what I would call it to Sophie who informed me that I was talking crap and in fact it was definitely the evening. By that time, whatever you want to call it, many of the others had left but Mike was still there and so were Watt and Harry despite it supposedly being the end of their two week session. Rambo would have to wait to see if he could move into the Island. I told him I would come back on Monday after work armed with food and boilies and wished him well.

Driving home, always an anti-climax, I felt a bit down. We had made no impression on Watt's lead and he was still in the best swim. Previously I would have been happy with the two mid doubles I had caught but I was now thinking what all women think, but are too gracious to tell us men with fragile egos, namely, that size is important. Whatever twenty pound plus equated to in inches made me like the woman who having pulled the pants down on her new capture was less than excited if it didn't break the desired statistical barrier. No matter that it was healthy, gave a good account of itself and had brought pleasure, it wasn't big enough and that was all there was to it!

From that Sunday the pace of things eased up dramatically amongst us warring SS members. Events had moved quickly up until now, revelation after revelation of wrong doing had come faster than cards turned by 'snap' players. That was over for a while and the ten of us settled down into a strange sort of agonised, untrusting normality as each affronted individual bided his time and waited to see what happened next and who done what. Of course we all fished as hard as we could for the TWTT and pulled as many wrinkles and cut as many corners as we thought we could safely get away with. In fact some of the strokes that were pulled in order to get another capture in the Tom Watt Twenty Log Book proved that initiative and creativity were alive and well in nineties Britain. Unfortunately honesty and decency were stiff on the mortuary slab.

Chapter 10

Monday at work crawled like an ant through treacle but eventually the nine hours of my life that I was wishing away elapsed. Off to the syndicate lake and don't spare the Escort 1.3 van! Rapture, an empty car park apart from Rambo's jalopy. Beside myself with excitement I rushed to join my mucker who was well and truly embedded in the Island swim, at last Watt had left the water and so had Harry. I dumped my gear in the Big Pads and went back to see Rambo. I wasn't taking any chances that someone would bowl up and nip in there while I was talking to him. I gave him the extra food he required and half of the boilies I had made on my week of wife induced absence. We had a quick chat and I mean quick, I was like a disobedient dog straining at an invisible leash to get fishing. Rambo could tell I was eager and dismissed me with a go and get'em wave of the arm. I ran to my swim cursing my lack of Linford Christie pace.

Like a lot of things in life, that evening turned out to be a let down. Mind you the mood of euphoria that had gripped me would have only been placated by at least three twenties, so maybe my hopes were a bit too optimistic. I had a common that just scraped ten pounds and one other run that pulled out virtually as I hit it. Two runs in a five hour stint was still reasonable going, many a time in seasons past I had blanked on summer evening sessions, so at least the bait seemed to be doing well.

Rambo had taken two fish since moving into the Island swim and he had another one that evening as well, all doubles but no Log Book entries. I left Rambo about ten that evening with my best Arnie impersonation telling him that 'I'll be back'.

The week that Rambo fished the Island was a very good week for him and by the end of it he had upped his total of twenties to eight, one ahead of Watt as far as we knew. As to myself, I became invigorated by Rambo's results and pushed myself and my relationship with Sophie to the limit. Knowing that I could share the Island with Rambo whenever I was around and benefit from his baiting up or pick from the other swims, made it a case of making hay while the sun shined. From Tuesday night onwards I was at the lake at about five in the afternoons, did the night and then trundled off to work at half seven in the morning and on the Friday I fished the whole weekend until six pm on the Sunday.

Now I have never been a great night time sleeper when fishing and what with the fair amount of action the pair of us were getting it wasn't too long before I felt and looked totally shot away. Rambo could kip it out during the slow periods of the day but I was on site working, in the loosest sense of the word anyway. I was more a physical presence than a sentient being and was soon nicknamed 'the zombie electrician' by the wags at work. Questions that enquired whether or not I was going to carry my tool kit around in the bags under my eyes were ignored simply on the grounds that to answer them required some form of brain function and unfortunately my neurones were out to lunch.

My production slumped as did my standing with the boss but to be honest his lectures about me getting my act together fell on deaf ears. By Sunday the effort had been worth it, I too, was up to a ground shaking eight on the TWTT Richter scale.

By eight pm on the Friday it had been another full house, but this time I was unaffected. I asked Rambo to tell Tom what the pair of us had caught as I didn't feel like talking to him, he didn't mind and was only too pleased to tell of our rising superiority. Luckily Tradders had done a few evenings and could verify our catches, the decision to sack fish rather than just witness each others so as to avoid any possible hassle had been worth it. That weekend Watt, Harry and Mike all struggled. Rambo and I had the Island and Big Pads respectively, we felt as if the pendulum had swung back in our favour.

From that third week of the season our bait gradually seemed to get better and produce more chances. The pair of us were fishing as much as we could, for the first three weeks Rambo had been there full time and even after that the pair of us fished weekends, loads of overnighters and the odd evening and morning when circumstances dictated. Consequently our bait was being fed in very regularly, even when we left the water we always put out a hundred or so boilies just as a parting gesture. As we entered the middle of July it became blatantly clear that we had the best bait on the water. Watt's bait, the Tropicano, seemed to get less effective as time went on.

Now I am no bait buff and will leave you the reader to draw your own conclusions as to why, despite similar amounts of quantities, our boilie's results improved and Watt and Co's subsided. Without giving too much away I would say that our bait was a better quality one, it should have been the money it cost us, well cost Rambo! Also it was clearly a bait that the carp liked the taste of. Watt's bait had held its own for a few weeks but then tailed off, it was as good as ours to begin with so the carp definitely liked it and yet longer term ours was better. A case of nutritional recognition? Maybe, who can say what actually does go on under water but above it we were winning the boilie war and as far as I was concerned that was the one fact that really mattered to me. Let the powers that be theorise as to why something happens, it just addles my brain and confuses me more when I try. Perhaps that was why I was never that good at carp fishing until Rambo came along with his boilie made in heaven and opened up a whole new world to me. The world of capturing carp regularly and even weirder, expecting to.

Rambo and I fished hard all through July although his full time fishing came to an end because of some mysterious business that he had to attend to. Apparently he was not going to become a hired mercenary but had other irons in the fire which he would not disclose. All I knew was that they must be important to drag him away when we were on a roll. For my part I soon found out that I simply couldn't cope with fishing the nights all week, it was beginning to make me feel really ill, purely from sleep deprivation I guess. I cut it down to a couple of all nighters a week and evening sessions the rest of the working week. As usual weekends were for fishing. Sophie had all but given up moaning about my general state of mind and attitude and stupidly I thought that her silence equated with, while not exactly approval, at least acceptance of my now slightly moderated efforts. I know now that she had in fact simply given up hope and at that time our relationship was close to its nadir but it would get worse.

During this period when I was at the lake I kept myself very much to myself especially if Rambo wasn't around. I didn't speak to either Watt, Harry, Mike or Dave and Tony once and luckily I didn't need to. When I had to get a witness for what was my tenth twenty Kipper was around to do the honours as he had been for the ninth one, it was just a case of waking him up. I found that the most effective method for this was a monkey climber poked into one of his auditory canals and wiggled around. Although there was temptation to ram it through his eardrum and skewer his brain (a feat no doubt equivalent to splitting the atom) and make off with his wallet as small recompense for what he had ripped off of me, I managed to resist. Kipper would grumble a bit but the old boy did what I asked him and consequently Watt got the bad news (to him) second hand.

I imagined Watt to be whining at him for witnessing my fish but Kipper could hardly refuse to do that for me although he could have played possum on his bedchair. The cold touch of stainless steel needle put paid to that. I was convinced that had I succumbed and shoved the needle right through his head and it had come out the other ear I could have slid the isotope on to the needle (rather than run off with his wallet), rocked his head from side to side and watched it go up and down through his eyes like in Tom and Jerry and still missed his brain. If only you could do things like that.

By the start of August, Rambo and I were sure that we were pulling out a fair old lead over Watt and his cronies but we were uncertain as to the exact scores on the doors because of our virtual isolation. Only Tradders had offered snippets of information but he hadn't been seen for the last few weeks, the others had sent us to Coventry. I was sure that any shit that Watt had flung in our direction was now sticking much easier because of the fact that we were outfishing everybody else comfortably. We were easier to dislike because of our success. However, the only way we could be certain as to our overall standing was to go to the bi-monthly meetings at the Black Horse and find out.

August the 10th was the next one and Rambo insisted that we go. If it had been at a time when he was away doing whatever he was doing I don't think that I would have gone but with him with me I felt as if I could cope with tension. In the past the meetings had been good fun, everyone was fairly buoyant and light hearted. To put it into boilie terms the meetings were like a sweet flavoured pop-up but that night the boilie was a large solid ball of semolina that had embedded itself in some foul silt. The atmosphere was heavy and it all stank, it really was crap. The only people to talk to me were Kipper and Tencher and even then only to grunt 'hello'. Poor old

Rambo never had a word uttered in his direction but I don't think he lost any sleep over it. Tradders was conspicuous by his absence. Watt played his hand cleverly by being exceptionally genial to everyone apart from us and in return Mike (what a two faced bastard), Harry, Dave and Tony played up to it. It was just a pathetic attempt to underline our ostracised situation and make us feel right out of it, which I suppose it did.

After the normal bits and bobs we heard the information that we needed, Watt read aloud from his Twenty Log book the scores, sizes and witnesses. I had ten (good), Rambo eleven (even better), Watt seven (ha! ha! still stuck on my lucky seven) Harry six (not enough matey), Dave five and Tony five (this raised a few eyebrows especially as each capture had been witnessed by the other and vice versa), Mike two (too much time spent shagging with Watt's wife) and the rest yet to get out the blocks, although Tencher had taken the lakes first six pound tench. Bully for him. Again I was thankful at the wisdom of whenever possible getting someone else to witness my fish apart from Rambo and him likewise, at least at the moment no-one could cock an eyebrow at us on that front. After all that Watt gave us 'an early days yet, long way to go' football managers speech and then out of the blue suddenly asked Rambo what it felt like to be in the lead and whether he could cope with the pressure of being there to be shot at, at the top of the pile.

"I'm just taking each twenty as it comes, but at the moment I'm obviously over the moon, Brian," said Rambo with a smirk on his face.

God knows what Watt was expecting him to say but the answer was clever enough to stop him in his tracks. Watt grunted a few comments that made it plain that he considered this a temporary aberration and that he was merely in second gear but would soon be putting his foot hard down and then he closed the meeting. Retire downstairs for drinks if you so desire. All the weird goings on and not a mention of even one of them from anyone, I couldn't believe it. Nothing about the draw rigging, the damaged cars, the police, the note, Harry's incident and having a word with the farmer about it, nothing. Not a thing.

Now you may ask why I didn't query the money situation that the farmer had told me about or about the prebaiting which were exclusive to my and Rambo's knowledge, and I will tell you. You see it was simply this, we were winning and we were happy to go with the flow and all the skulduggery as long as no-one attempted to oust us from the syndicate because of it. If we had dropped the bombshell about Watt and Kipper ripping us all off, regardless of whether we were believed or not it could have created a situation that might just have caused enough upheaval to deprive us of our ultimate goal. That goal was to beat Watt for the Trophy and let him have to write about it. We just wanted to defeat him and then let the other fools who at the moment sheltered under his wing know what sort of bloke he really was. If we rocked the boat that chance might be taken away from us and of course if we started to lose the competition we could exercise our right to dump Watt in the shit whenever we liked. I was still sure that we held enough aces to cover any eventualities.

The only thing that concerned me was how the others had closed shop and stuck together. Dave and Tony knew about Mike's adultery, they had caused Harry's incident, damaged the cars, made up the note and yet because of the non landing of a fish now sat fairly and squarely on the side of their previous victims. Maybe they did have cold feet about all the aggro and just saw an opportunity to get out of what they had done and blame it all on me and Rambo. Luckily there was no real way that they could accuse us particularly with some of them knowing what we knew, well not without causing mayhem amongst themselves when we let a few cats out of the bag. Perhaps this was the reason for their tactic of trying to make us out as lepers. Being unable to nail the dirty deeds on us they were trying to make it so uncomfortable and intimidating that we would leave of our own accord or simply not fish as much. With me it might have worked but surely they had enough brains to realise that a gorilla armed with a baseball bat wouldn't intimidate Rambo and that he had ample gumption for two and could pull me through.

Overall the picture was grim and I think that if we had been a family rather than a syndicate half of us would have been taken into care. Rambo would never be released back into the community and we would have been the subject of a Social Services seminar. A bloke with a beard, duffel coat and sandals would pronounce us socially wanting and a classic case of what today's materialistic and non-caring society could produce. Collectively, he would claim, that we epitomised the culture of victimhood. It was not our fault, not of our making, we were not responsible for our own actions and we were merely puppets dancing to the tune of external influences that had so corrupted us. We would be sent away on a tax payer sponsored rehabilitation holiday, somewhere hot with easy access to mug 50lb carp with all tackle and bait supplied, except for Watt and Kipper. They would be shut away for ten years on an incest charge for screwing the rest of us.

Rambo was made ever more determined by the realisation that things had panned out as I had said after the landing net fracas with Dave i.e. them against us. It seemed to fortify him, I suppose anybody who has been a mercenary thrives on aggro, it must be a sort of job requirement. On the CV under personality the words 'enjoys a good punch up' must improve your chances of getting the job and it certainly seemed the case with him. Naturally our isolation pushed us closer together and Rambo opened up much more to me and told me things about himself that he hadn't before. The most important item being that his new workload that had eaten into his fishing was none other than a bit of illegal weapon running. What with his mass of military contacts from army days and from his 'foreign holidays' as he called his mercenary fighting, he knew enough shady characters to act as a very useful go between.

He now had a sort of selling job. A kind of killing tool sales representative. 20 dozen AK 47's? Certainly sir,and what colour? Now I mention this little side show because it affected me in two ways, one was that Rambo would and had been out of the country for periods of time and therefore I was left to fight the lone fight for a while and secondly Rambo said that if the deal came off he would be more flush than five diamond cards in a game of poker. This meant loads of bait and any other goodies that he felt could influence the TWTT into our arms. Ahh the benefits of a benevolent sponsor!

It was on one of the days towards the latter end of August when Rambo was expected back that I happened to be passing close by the lake. I had just been to an emergency call out where some brain dead householder had decided to hang a picture directly above a power point having forgotten that his re-wire had meant chases in the wall down from the first floor joist space to all sockets because of a solid ground floor. With skill he had hit the cable and nearly frightened himself to death before fusing his ring main. Anyway this call out gave me a bit of time to juggle with so I nipped into the car park to see if Rambo was back and fishing. His car wasn't there but Dave and Tony's two were, so I decided to nip down and have a sly gander at what they were up to.

I wandered down the path expecting them to be sharing the Island swim and sure enough they were. To be honest I wanted to spy on them, I was sure that the pair of them were pulling a few strokes as there was no way that I reckoned that they had managed to pull out ten twenties between them. I left the path and circled around in the trees to the swim to the left, the Deep Corner, and lay down in good cover to watch them for a while. I started to scan them with a pair of binoculars that Rambo had given me, ex-army of course and acknowledged my correct intuition. Between them the bastards had ten rods out in what looked like an attempt to cover virtually every good spot on the lake. They all angled off in various directions, the outer rods which were on single rod rests were a good twenty yards from their legal rack of three allowing them to hit areas that would be impossible from the rack.

Suddenly I saw Tony start running to one of his outer rods, although I couldn't hear anything it seemed obvious he had a take. As I focused in on the rod I could see the monkey climber pogoing up and down and the reel backwinding (the poor dears couldn't afford baitrunners, no wonder they'd spent all their money on rods!). Well the fish kited around towards the mass of rods and pretty soon it was knit one purl one as it picked up other lines and started more churners. I had to laugh as Dave was frantically dipping rods and then lifting them up so that Tony could walk over or underneath them as the fish shot down amongst all the other lines. Tony hobbled and tripped over the rods like the world's worst hurdler or walked into them giving them the Glasgow handshake as he tried to track the fish rather than look where he was going. A couple of times Dave dipped when he should have lifted as the fish went underneath the line rather than over the top as he had presumed, then Tony had to back track and get under the rod that the fish had picked up. To top it all he had just managed to make it down to about rod number six when the fish started going back up the other way so they went through the whole palaver again.

Eventually two lines must have become hopelessly tangled because I saw Dave put them on their rests and open the bale arms and he stopped trying to manipulate them clear. I was convinced that it was just a matter of time before excessive side strain from the two snagged terminal leads caused a pull out when Dave reached for the net and crouched down in readiness. Inside me some nasty part of me hoped it would come off and that they would lose it. (Hands up everyone who can honestly say that at some stage in their fishing career they have not been disappointed to see somebody lose a fish. A quick head count....... just three...... and all of them liars!)

After some rather frantic action close in I was amazed to see Dave move with the net and lift up a sizeable lump of carp. If only he had known that I was watching he would have no doubt told me that, 'that was the way to do it'. The pair of them went about the unhooking and weighing of the fish under my watchful gaze and soon the camera made its appearance. I was pretty sure that the fish was large enough for Watt's log book and this capture would put Tony up to half a dozen twenties. He looked rightly chuffed as Dave snapped away. They put the fish back in the sling and then started to walk down to my swim, at first I thought that they were just going to put the fish back away from their base camp but this was not the case. The pair of them walked past me and down to the Big Pads, Tony had the weigh sling with carp and the camera and Dave had a sports holdall with him which he must have taken from his bivvy.

Once at the Big Pads Dave held the fish while Tony took the photos, they put the fish back in the sling and then to my complete bewilderment the pair of them stripped off and each put on a set of different clothes that had been in the sports holdall. Then they marched off down to the Pines and took photos of each other with the fish again only this time they took the photos well under cover using a flash whereas all the other snaps had been out in the bright sunlight. I didn't need to be the brain of Britain to realise that Dave and Tony now had seven twenties each courtesy of an amazing repeat capture coincidence of both catching the same fish twice. In fact given my scepticism I was prepared to wager that it was highly likely that the other fish caught before might also have something to do with repeat captures. Talk about making a little go a long way. (Just as a point of interest out of the ten twenties I had caught so far only one had been a repeat and out of our total of 21 -Rambo's 11- four fish were the same. Repeat captures hadn't been quite so prominent as I had thought they might be, I suppose this spoke volumes about how prolific our lake had become and what a good strain of carp we had).

Dave and Tony's little ploy was a neat trick to play if you were that desperate but how many times could you realistically play it without giving the game away? To be totally convincing you needed a bigger choice of fish. For a moment I imagined Watt, Harry, Mike and Kipper were all embroiled in a twenty-go-round, callously snapping each others twenties and running up a log book score quicker than how calendar dates fall off in front of your eyes in old movies to show the passage of time. When Tony put the fish back into its home and rung out the weigh sling I knew that the pair of them were doing this off their own backs. If they had been running a carp cartel they'd have sacked it and waited for the next punter to turn up and have his portrait taken with an increasingly over-handled carp.

I waited for the pair of them to get settled and then crept back to the path, I was about to head back to the car park when a wave of ill will coupled to some strong self-confidence bestowed itself upon me and I started to walk back down to the lake. I was going to test how good their early warning radar system was. I stomped down the path and started to whistle quietly, a familiar tune associated with seven vertically challenged Disney cartoon characters. I started to sing some words under my breath. "Hi ho, hi ho, the extra rods must go - So wind them back or be in the cack - Hi ho, hi ho, hi ho, hi ho." Not exactly Bob Dylan or whoever you consider to be good at lyrics but there you go.

I walked on purposefully, my eyes staring for the first sign of them hearing me. I got to within about 200 yards before I spotted that I had been spotted, then there was a flurry of activity that I could vaguely make out through the foliage between myself Dave and Tony. Undoubtedly they were feverishly winding in the four snide rods after having made the horrendous decision of which ones to leave out and which ones to pull in. In my mind's eye I could picture a large twenty just about to suck in one of their baits when all of a sudden it was whisked away from under its nose, while the baits they left out never had a carp within 50 yards. You can only hope can't you?

 Casually I strode down to the Wide swim, the one to the right of the Island where they were, and stood on the bankside. Under the pretension of surveying the lake I took out my binoculars and looked far and wide also taking in the pair of them. Quickly I counted a legit six rods but I could also see a couple of rod tips poking out of their bivvy, they had halved the rogue four and shoved them out of sight only not very carefully because of the panic I had caused. I carried on looking for maybe twenty seconds and then packed away the binoculars turned on my heel and pushed off. I could only guess at how pissed off they were that they had had to pull in all because of me showing up for about one minute and then going. However much it had got to them it wasn't enough. I knew that they would cast out again eventually but they would have to worry about if I was coming back with my gear and hopefully it would put them on edge. Anyway for a few minutes of my time I had caused them a fair bit of hassle. Vindictive? You bet!

I left the car park and returned to work hoping that Rambo would soon be back from a lucrative trip. Maybe I could persuade him that I needed a complete brand new kit to help in my efforts to thwart Watt or if not that at least a new bivvy with full central heating, it would soon be Autumn and starting to get chilly.

Halfway through September Watt's article about the syndicate appeared on the hallowed pages of Carpworld. I read it of course and I also tried to read between the lines. Watt mentioned his bait and I wondered whether a little bit of commercialism had been his reason for using a shop-bought. A bit of free bait for some favourable publicity? Possibly, and why not? Every other sport has sponsorship, players get paid to wear this type of football boot, to play with that type of racket or golf club, it's the way of the world so why should fishing be any different? Watt had used the bait and had caught what he had said that he had caught on the bait, so fair enough if you ask me, for once I had no argument with him. If Mr Shimano had asked me to try out some reels of his I wouldn't say no that's for sure. To be honest I'd be happy to be given a couple of free swivels but even then I'd probably be over sponsored for the talent I have. After all is said and done you pays your money and takes your choice, you chose whether you believe what you read.

The other blatant thing to come across (to myself, not to the casual reader) was the niggle between yours truly, Rambo and Watt, but that was an item firmly between the lines. There was no mention of any of the funny business, unsurprisingly Watt never mentioned how he had rigged the draw and prebaited or that he omitted to give a detailed balance sheet of the financial status of the syndicate and how much money he was making out of it. There was no mention of Harry having his cables cut or of the damage to the cars. There was no reference to strange notes stuck to bivvies, no reference to rows over netting fish and moreover there was no reference to me or Rambo. Everyone else got a name check while the pair of us got the 'another member' treatment, the git also missed out most of our fish. To counter balance the omissions we had loads of reminders about the skill of the author. Most laughable was the move from the Island to the Oak when Rambo had moved his gear back to stop him getting in his pocket and had inadvertently put him on the fish. I quote; 'Suddenly I noticed a bow wave from the bay area, quickly I fetched my binoculars and trained a keen eye on the surface. Sure enough I spotted more fish starting to move out and decided it was most definitely time to relocate and try and intercept them even though I was in what was considered the best swim in the lake. Perhaps others would have been loathe to move from such a swim but experience had taught me......' and on he went to describe his success. Then of course came my big moment when I had arrived back after the sex show between Mike and Jennifer to be told by Watt himself that I had bombed out big time, '.... one member who had left the water for a couple of hours could hardly believe that I had in fact caught two twenties in the short time he had been gone.....' etc etc ad nauseam.

To the uninitiated it was an interesting read but it wasn't a true reflection of events, not a warts and all job, not like you are reading now. I also think that if anyone within the syndicate had any doubts about the tensions between Watt and ourselves the article subtly dispelled them, we had been given the cold shoulder no two ways about it. Watt had left the article open to be able to update on the TWTT at around January time and promised to let everyone know how many he was winning by. The only problem being was that now, he wasn't. If Rambo and I could keep our noses in front up until around November when the article presumably would have to be submitted by, Watt was going to have to do some very clever wriggling not to have his thunder stolen. Now that would make an even more interesting read from my view point.

Chapter 11

Golden Autumn's touch fell upon the syndicate lake and I'm not just talking about the leaves. A certain type of fish, around which this tale of mayhem is constructed, lent a similar hue to the overall picture as they fell constantly to our rods and showed their beauty. Fittingly it seemed that either myself or Rambo would metaphorically collect a medal of that colour in the TWTT race although cheapskate Watt had only run to a silver trophy. As the fish started to put on even more weight for the winter so the pair of us put daylight between ourselves and the opposition in terms of twenties on the bank. It was heady stuff, even our testosterone producing equipment was rumoured to be golden.

Rambo had returned from his weapons seminar full of good cheer and more importantly a lot richer than when he had left. Although not party to the full S.P on what had happened Rambo had confirmed that all had gone very well and that he was in a position to fund our attempted humiliation of Watt very generously. A measure of how lucrative his underworld dealings must have been was reflected in the fact that he bought me three new Delkims after one of my old Optonics died from a massive circuit coronary that not even the technical application of a rubber bivvy mallet could cure.

"It was just a simple case of it being burnt out," I had jokingly bragged to him, "pure over-use. The poor old thing just couldn't take the pace of all those belting runs."

He had laughed, so had I, but after fiddling with the damn thing for over an hour and still not managing to get it going I resorted to the 'when-in-doubt-or-all-else-fails-hit-the-bloody-thing-with-a-hammer' mentality and my laughing had stopped. The Optonic had taken on a new form, that of a three dimensional jigsaw, batteries included, plural for the Duracell inside and the physical retribution that I had taken out on it as in 'assault and...'

Carp fishing without a buzzer. A concept too hideous to contemplate. I had immediately thought of Tradders and his bits of silver paper and the effort and concentration involved which in turn reminded me that he hadn't been seen for ages.

The first run I had on my new alarms turned out to be my fourteenth twenty and a new personal best. The fish was Cyril the one I had taken right at the start of the season but it had increased in weight by just over three pounds and had whacked my Avons down to 28lb 2ozs. I was jubilant. The fish came out from the Big Pads in the last week of September on a Saturday when Watt, Harry, Mike, Dave and Tony had all been there. I bet they just loved it that they could actually say that they were there on the day the lake record was broken. If I had later gone up to each one of them individually and stuck two fingers up at them, you know right up close to their faces and tore open their nostrils while I was at it, it would have had maybe only 10% of the impact of me catching that fish in their presence.

Tencher had landed and weighed Cyril for me, all very meticulously as it happens and I had thanked him accordingly. Tencher and I were just about on speaking terms despite him having fallen out with Rambo and I was happy enough for him to help me. I guess that I was so wrapped up in the actual capture that I failed to notice the sly trick he had pulled until I was actually unhooking my rig from the landing net mesh. It was then that I retraced the whole event using what I laughingly refer to as my memory, (I suffer from the looking for keys that are in my pocket syndrome).

I had unhooked the fish while Tencher had stood a respectful distance away and as far as my memory was concerned I was sure that the boilie had survived the tussle and was still on the hair. I had then got my sling, laid it over the fish and gone about the whole routine, with Tencher's help, of weighing and photographing (a new record 20 snaps, well one record deserves another) the fish. It was only after all this when, still in a state of high euphoria, with Tencher off to inform Watt of another shattering body blow to go in his Twenty Log Book that the case of the missing boilie came to light. If my own recollections were to be trusted Tencher had palmed our wonder boilie away from under my nose and it was no doubt being subjected to dissection, chemical analysis and thorough autopsy by Dr Tom Watt.

Tencher had earnt his thirty pieces of silver, or whatever Watt had rewarded him like some modern day Judas but it was unlikely he would become over burdened with guilt and top himself. All the guilt was laden on myself for what appeared to be a large error of personal judgement on my part.

As I said before it was from about the fourth week of the season when our bait superiority came truly to the fore and the pair of us realised that it was this rather than great fishing or rigs that was giving us the big leg-up. At that time as our bait got better so Watt and his merry crew started to feel the pinch with a declining Tropicano, the combination of one going up and another going down seemed conducive towards encouraging skulduggery and Rambo and myself had started to take steps to keep our secret. Although there had been no attempts, as far as could be seen, of underhand activities to find out about our bait we had noticed the odd pair of binoculars on us when casting. At pinch they could discern the colour, red, as I told you much earlier but so what? Hardly any use whatsoever, it was just as likely that they were looking to see where we were casting and what sort of rig we were using. You just have to except that you can't keep catching from a certain spot, well known or otherwise, without people seeing it. Well, not unless you erected some sort of hoarding around you and the area of water you could fish to, I expect Nashy already makes it and with his name on the side like some giant advertising poster.

Anyway we decided that as things were fairly competitive and acrimonious to say the least we would step up precautions in a moderate way. We hadn't baited up with any of the others in close proximity and certainly hadn't put on any hook baits. We were meticulous with free offerings especially about leaving them around on the bank if they had fallen out of the catty sling and of course they were tucked away in the bivvy in bags for the rest of the time. If I had popped to see Rambo from a distant swim I had even taken them with me so that no one could sneak into my bivvy and grab a couple. Obviously I had underestimated the lengths that they would go to even to the extent of getting someone outside their clique to do the dirty deed for them and in such an underhand manner when I was at my most vulnerable. i.e. on cloud nine. To me it reeked of forethought and planning which showed how bad things were. Of course that statement could just be paranoia and Tencher could have simply been a maverick trying to get Watt brownie points. Either way the deed had been done.

I ran through it all again in my mind and was certain that things had happened how I recollected. Bleating to either Tencher or Watt about my suspicions seemed pointless as a straight denial was inevitable and I couldn't prove otherwise. All that it seemed that I could do was to go and tell Rambo the great news and expect a severe ear bashing and either a bill for the new alarms or a request to have them given back. Strangely I got neither and rather than being niggled with me he seemed more upset with himself.

"Shit!" He had exclaimed. "Oh God, Matt. I'm sorry, I should have realised what was happening and warned you to be on guard."

"What are you on about?" I asked somewhat flummoxed.

"Well, a couple of days ago I went out early morning to find my dustbin had been upended and the rubbish slung all over the place. I had just thought that it was a fox having a rummage for some old leftovers or something. Now with this happening I reckon that it wasn't a fox but a big rat."

"A rat?" I said screwing my nose up, not really understanding his gist.

"Yeah. A syndicate rat. A rat looking through my rubbish for old bait mix bags and flavour bottles."

"Christ! Do you think that they're that desperate to find out, then? I mean pawing through somebody's rubbish in the middle of the night is a bit sad isn't it." Rambo nodded. I then asked the $64,000 question. "Was there anything in there that you had chucked out from any bait making? There can't be can there? We haven't made any for well over a week." I said as much in hope as anything.

"Huh! Unfortunately I did sling out a couple of old flavour bottles a little while ago and one of the enhancers as well."

"Oh, bollocks!" I said deflated.

"Absolutely. They were ones I found down by the side of the cooker, they must have been the originals from the first bait making session. I never even gave it a thought I just slung them in the bin. Our only chance is that the dustmen had emptied that bin of rubbish before our night prowler had his little nose around. I can't remember exactly when I threw the old bottles out, see."

"So as a worst case scenario they have the boilie, the flavour and the enhancer?" I said somewhat gutted.

"Yep." Said Rambo. "Watt will certainly be able to tell what type the base mix is even if he can't tell whose it is and to be honest I doubt whether that is particularly crucial. What with the flavour and enhancer he's got 90% of the story. Again the 10% he doesn't know, is it that vital? I reckon that whatever they come up with it will be good enough to hitch a ride on our boilie's bandwagon. With winter on the way we may have to alter our bait slightly in any case and any distinction between the two baits, if perceptible in the first place, will probably be lost then. I think that we will just have to accept that our edge has been severely blunted. To be positive about it all we have to do is match them out until March. Actually we don't even need to do that with the lead we've got, so we're still in the driving seat."

"Yeah, but I bet we'll have to look in the mirror a lot more than we have done to see Watt looming large in a Lamborgini Diablo," I said ruefully.

"Don't forget boy, we're still in a Ferrari. One each in fact."

Rambo was right of course, both of us had a healthy gap between ourselves and Watt, while Rambo still had a two fish advantage over myself. I guess it was my natural pessimism that made me get the jitters, that coupled with the fact that I felt foolish at how easily Tencher had duped me when I was in ecstasy. The snide whelp, taking advantage of a defenceless, euphoria saturated, just caught a PB, carp fisherman. There ought to be a law against it but the only one that appeared to be in play was Sod's and that said that the dustmen hadn't cleared the bin and the evidence was there for the syndicate rat to find. Time would tell.

Time marched on....... and time told. Firstly it told me that I now physically hated the rest of the syndicate members apart from Rambo and Tradders. I was very bitter to say the least, the best that could be said about this was that it fired me up to go fishing as much as I could and made me try as hard as I could. (This had other repercussion but more of that later). Fishing ceased to become a true pleasure but became more of a grave necessity, I had little time for anything else. Fishing had become a drug to me and without it I was definitely 'cold-turkey'. (I wonder if anyone does that in an EA flavour?). It occurred to me that maybe there were many others who had become so immersed in fishing that the whole reason for going in the first place had been lost to them as they endlessly ground out the hours playing the numbers game whether in size or quantity. The idea that you go fishing to avoid stress, to get pleasure, to get away from the rat race with all its monotony of having to do this that or the other, was blown away because that was what the fishing had become. It had become a job, instead of sales figures to meet there were twenty capture figures to meet. You had to be fishing 'X' hours a week and the desire for big, fat salaries was replaced by the desire to catch big, fat carp. The frustrations of work and the frustrations of fishing were one of the same because of the heavy emphasis of having to catch. Of course by that stage you're oblivious to all this. Time will tell but not until later and who knows what might have happened by then.

Later it became apparent that our boilie had been well and truly stolen but the spoils of the crime had not been evenly distributed among the other syndicate members. For all Watts attempts to run a solid embargo against Rambo and myself it seemed that there was still a higher echelon amongst our enemies. Through our binoculars in a cute piece of role reversal we spotted red boilies on the end of Watt, Harry and Mike's terminal tackle. Kipper, Dave and Tony were apparently kept in the dark. I wondered if Watt and his immediate cronies were to be as diligent at keeping what they had stolen as we had tried to be and whether a third party would try to take what the second party had nicked from us, the first party, but it only made my head hurt, so I gave up worrying about it. Tencher it seemed still had no interest in carp despite being so involved in the theft and as his mainly summer quarry became more elusive, so did he.

His duplicity was no doubt fuelled by his altercation with Rambo over the Little Pads swim months earlier rather than any desire to put carp on the bank. To be honest I was glad that he was around less as I could have cheerfully rammed my umbrella up his you know where and then had a bloody good go at trying to open it.

The fact that the big three (in their minds) had not passed the boilie on to the others suggested that one of them had been the phantom dustbin rummager - the syndicate rat. Somehow I just couldn't see Lord Almighty Watt getting his odious hands dirty on such a sleazy, underling type operation. I reckoned that it was Mike, he didn't seem to mind running his hands over other peoples' property .... or wife for that matter. Although it seemed that Watt had done very little in gaining info on our boilie apart from the admittedly crucial final analysis he was certainly the one who got the biggest boost. As time told yet again, Watt started to become the most successful angler on the lake.

With our boilie to arm him his superior (God that hurts) fishing ability started to scratch away at our lead. By the next bi-monthly meeting which was in the second week of October Rambo was still in the lead but the deficit was being cut. He had eighteen captures to his name, I had fifteen and Watt was making a move up the inside rail to reach twelve. Harry and Mike were also gaining ground (ten and nine respectively) and had by now overtaken Dave and Tony whose spectacular run of repeat captures by both of them, although backed by photographs, had made Watt raise his eyebrows so much that they nearly disappeared down the back of his neck. I was convinced that Watt knew that they had been pulling a fast one but chose to turn a blind eye to it in order to maintain collective solidarity against Rambo and myself. Of course I could have told him the whole sordid truth like I could about many things but the game plan was silence.

As things became tighter in the TWTT hunt so the tension increased and the desire to win likewise. We all seemed trapped in an unreal world, a microcosm of vicious intensity where fishing and catching twenty pound carp was simply the be all and end all, of everything. I had thought that I had reached the limits of my intensity over fishing but I found out much to my own personal cost that I had one more level to reach, namely the full time carp fisherman stage. Out of the blue on a Friday I was told that I had been made redundant because of a double lack of work.

No need to work my notice just to sling my hook, a fitting phrase I thought somewhat cynically.

One of the lack of work criteria was of the customer variety the other was a lack of production, my production. If I had been my old self, free from the demands of the TWTT hunt I am sure that someone else would have got the bullet before me but I had let my vocational priorities slip and had been rewarded with the gooner. After the initial shock and a whirling mind that spun giddily with the implications of fiscal survival and what my other half would say, a ray of hope descended through the blackness with laser like intensity. With redundancy, dole money and a bit of luck I could really go for the TWTT. Time, that most crucial commodity, was now on my side. My plan formed in my head as I drove home with my P45 for company, fish out the season until March and then get my head together and get a job. The last part of that sentence I can now see was a pure add on, if the truth were known I was almost glad to get the push. Together Rambo and I could virtually both fish full time and with that big bonus I couldn't see even Watt clawing back the deficit.

I shall spare you the details of the hideous row that I had with Sophie about my lifestyle plans for the next five months and how, with the reflexes of a rattle-snake (a fat, old one) I had dodged the flying crockery. Those of you who have kept up with this sorry tale will recall my mentioning the ultimate low point in my relationship with Sophie. It may be hard to imagine, as it was for myself as I ducked and dodged the ceramic missiles that were whistling about my ears, that in fact this wasn't it. There was one more step to be taken into the abyss when I paid the ultimate price by foregoing my liberty but that is the end of my story and needs to be told later.

By November 5th (I had no need for fireworks, the row with Sophie was enough to last me years) I was with Rambo fishing side by side, resolute in our determination for one of us to win. With a dug-in, trench mentality and jaws clamped tight like a pit bull on a postie's leg we epitomised steely determination. Rambo, rich from his dubious dealings proved himself to be a mate beyond most mates. He offered to pay my mortgage up until the end of the season if I made the boilies for the rest of the season, with the ingredients he supplied. It was a pretty fair exchange to say the least and it alleviated much pressure from my shoulders. Pathetically I thought that this also set the record straight, well straighter, with Sophie and my mind turned fully to the TWTT having rather ridiculously convinced myself that all was hunky-dory.

I don't know when it occurred to Watt that despite having purloined our boilie to get on a level footing for a short while the stakes had been upped again by the pair of us now free to commit ourselves full time. I suppose by about the fifth or sixth time he bowled up to the lake all at different times and we were there it probably dawned on him. He didn't ask of course, his ego wouldn't allow it. I suppose at the start of all this he was convinced he would win at a canter and shower himself in glory with all of us and the readers of Carpworld as he told of his stunning win by his own fair hand. I also reckoned that he thought that he could fish fairly leisurely on the syndicate lake and still have ample time to fish some of the circuit waters that he had dabbled with over the years. A bit of prebaiting, getting the right swim to start off with, that alone would see him right. The major flaw in his plan was the motivation of the opposition spurred on by the unveiling of his skulduggery at various points along the way. By the time that it had seeped into the self-absorbed brain of Tom Ya Man Watt that we were camped in and deadly serious for a hard winter's campaign he was probably wishing he had never thought of the TWTT as another supporting strut to his ego. It had all got out of hand and it seemed to me that his only chance of victory was to match us with equal commitment or pull another stroke, whatever that could be.

Rambo and I plugged on through a mild November with some success. Watt, Harry and Mike were doing their fair share of nights and all weekends while Dave and Tony nearly matched them. It was interesting to note that when Watt fished the night Mike didn't and vice-versa, Mike clearly found Jennifer preferential to a night stuck in a bivvy. Poor old Watt, you just had to laugh, him out in the cold while Mike was romping with his wife and yet he obviously had no inclination of what was going on, he just didn't associate the fact that when he was fishing and not at home Mike never showed. It crossed my mind that I wasn't at home very much and Sophie wasn't exactly enamoured with our relationship but I knew my wife wouldn't cheat on me. Watt probably thought the same! Kipper showed up on the odd weekend and when Rambo called him up on the new mobile phone he had bought so that he could witness any twenties we caught. We wanted no ambiguity on that front and Kipper never complained about being asked so it worked out fine. Tencher and Tradders were never seen. I could understand why Tencher might bow out in the colder weather but Tradders had always done a bit in winter so that remained a mystery.

It was about the first week in December that the gauntlet the pair of us had hurled down was finally picked up. Watt and Harry stayed after a weekend, all week in fact and the next weekend and the next week they stayed as well. It was full time fishing for them as well. They too had finally succumbed to the inevitable fact that if you don't put the hours in you can never hope to compete with those that do. What sacrifices both financial and domestic they had made could only be guessed at but it meant that this was a serious business, it would go to the wire.

The very fact that they were there somehow seemed, even if it was perversely, to make it better. If we had won without a fight it could have been dismissed as a triumph of pure grind over skill but now that we were finally on a level footing they had put their reputations on the line in a no excuses conflict.

The fact that I could look out across no-mans land as I chose to call the area between the Island where we were camped and the Big Pads where the enemy lay and actually see the foe focused my mind on the reasons for being there. It had come down to this two against two in a final slog to the bitter end. The others had become mere peripherals, bit part players. No quarter was asked or given, we were the two superpowers, virtually the same technology at our disposal, definitely a cold war between us locked in a conflict to seize superiority. We were the world ten years ago, me and Rambo- America. God on our side, all shining star spangled banner, capitalism and democracy. Watt and Harry the loathsome Commies with their corrupt regime and their satellites held together by lies, deceit, fear and the Red Army. Would they crumble and embrace our system and ultimately fail as had happened or would we wilt under their heinous onslaught? The question intrigued me as I sat gazing out at three newish Delkims that the money of capitalism had bought me. Naturally there was another alternative, there usually is. Armageddon. Mutually assured destruction, but on that day sitting on my bedchair by a lake of a few acres, I couldn't really see that. To paraphrase an old saying, there's none so blind as those that can't see.

Chapter 12

As December wore on and neared Christmas my mind turned not to carols, tinsel, presents, glad tidings, family re-unions and loads of toy advertisements but to.. Ok let's be honest it didn't turn at all, it stayed like it had for the last six months on catching twenty pound carp to win a grotty silver trophy that I could have gone out and bought for about £50. But of course it's not so much the actual materialistic value but the thought that counts. The thought that associated itself with the TWTT was stuffing Watt's ego and all his nasty dealings right down his gullet with the added incentive that he might choke on it and ultimately die. Tis the season to be jolly, tra-la-la-la-la..la-la-la-laa. Bollocks to all that, this was war. It was them or us. Only one set of reputations could come out of this alive, we were all in too deep to say it meant nothing and that we could walk away defeated and uncut. Victory was a must.

Since the four of us had decided to go full time the feelings within the syndicate had changed subtly. Whereas before we had been ostracised by the rest, the cold clammy hand of dislike had also fallen on Watt and Harry. Had the other members realised their folly at trying to out Rambo and myself and seen the error of their ways? Ha! No, the reasons for the four of us getting almost equal amounts of disdain were much more base. Quite simply the four of us in our two pairs were hogging the two best swims on the lake and the constant occupation of them was bugging, to put it mildly, the others.

Tencher had come back on the scene as had Tradders, the first with a strange new-found desire to carp fish! I mean !!! The second re-appearing after a long period when he had hoped that all 'this silly competitive nonsense would be over'. Fat chance. Dave and Tony were forever griping, probably because they realised that they were now a pair of nothings again and could not hope to be an influence on the TWTT for all their previous conniving efforts. Kipper actually seemed annoyed as well, maybe he was losing sleep over it and Kipper seemed to rate sleep above all else. It was only dear old Mike who saw the humour in it. He would be forever coming around asking how the war was going, if one of us had died from exposure or boredom and when was the last time either of us felt human. He loved it, virtually 100% uninterrupted access to Watt's wife and the chance to come round and take the piss whenever he wanted and do a bit fishing. Perfect.

It was Mike who had erected the scoreboard in the Deep Corner, the swim in-between the Island and Big Pads. The names on it were Harry, Matt, Rambo and Tom, alphabetical order, and to the right of each name was a number, the crucial number which told how many twenties that individual had caught. At that time before Christmas it read 14, 20, 23 and 17 respectively.

"It'll be ideal," he had told Rambo and myself. "All you need to do is wander down into no-man's land and see how the war is going." He laughed. I knew he was enjoying this. "I'll check out the log book as much as I can and collate the results and put them up on the scoreboard so you can see how things are going. You can check it out when you want then. You won't have restless nights worrying about whether or not the last fish you saw the enemy catch was a twenty or not. Equally they won't be able to send out mis-information via the grapevine. I suppose it wouldn't be necessary if you were prepared to witness each others' fish but I know that you won't want to do that. I mean parley with the foe. Preposterous."

"Just make sure you do the weighing all fair and square, or whoever does it, does it fair and square," I said.

"Hmm. That's a point. Mike paused and then had a sudden inspiration. I know, what we'll do is this. Whoever gets to weigh in a twenty has to get one member of the opposing pair to witness it on the scales, and we'll use just one pair of scales. I mean obviously you won't want to walk into the enemy camp unarmed so we'll do it in the Deep Corner. Just to be on the safe side I think you ought to be flying a white hanky when you come down though."

"Very good," I said, "most amusing."

And so it was that each pair of us took it in turns to go down to the Deep Corner at any time night or day to witness the weight of a twenty pound fish which had been caught by one of the other pair but witnessed and originally weighed by a third party. This was our equivalent to the world's weaponry destruction verification. It must have been hilarious to watch a real miserable, grumpy, dishevelled carp fisherman trudge down to a swim just to give an ungracious nod to the weigher that it was indeed a twenty. What made it worse of course was that you knew that the other pair were high fiving it in their swim and cracking open the bubbly. It was a long walk there and back.

That then was the state of play, four members slugging it out life or death style. Five members getting the hump and one member having a whale of a time. I suppose that now I'm cleared of the madness of the TWTT it's clear that Mike had the best attitude of us all, but I had lost all rationality and was a one track person, like three others.

Fishing full time with Rambo was a weird experience, just fishing full time would have been odd enough, but with him it nudged it that bit further. Although I was desperate to outdo Watt I honestly think that I would have gone barmy on my own and probably caved in. (Ok so I might have been barmy in any case but you know what I mean). Rambo had a strength of purpose that just rubbed off onto you, when the chips were down he was great to have at your side. The long hours of inactivity were always shortened by his recollections of past deeds, he had some horrendous tales to tell about things he'd seen and done.

He was quite a character once you got to know him and boy did I get to know him. I had the time to. He told me how he got his nickname, Rambo, and it was well before Stallone came along. Named at birth Timothy Eugene Ramsbottom by unwise parents he had insisted on being called Ramsbo which being rather odd to get your tongue around had mutated into Rambo at junior school. The film connection was pure coincidence, Rambo had always been military minded. It seemed to encapsulate his rather strange life of which I was now a part of. He was just different, he was so different that he kept two live hand grenades in his rucksack 'just in case'.

"Just in case, what?!" I had asked him after nearly dying of fright having accidentally come across them looking for his boilies.

"You never know when they might come in handy."

"Aren't you worried about the pins coming out?" I had asked him turning rather pale.

"No, but you are."

"Well, now I know they're there, yeah."

"Don't worry about it, I'll smother the blast with my body," he had said winking.

The days rolled on and became shorter and the nights ever longer. I had got used to night fishing by pure necessity but I still preferred the day, at least now I could sleep them out if somewhat fitfully. December 21st the shortest day came and went, the next day I went home for more provisions and more bait and to sign on as I had to every two weeks. I found a note from Sophie saying that she was going to stay with her Mum and Dad for Christmas and as I hadn't told her whether I was going to carry on fishing or come home I could please myself what I done. I felt a tinge of remorse and regret which rapidly left me as I knew that I could fish on and had been saved the hassle of convincing myself that it was all right to do so and telling Sophie about it. Christmas was only another day after all but to mark it I bought a few cans of lager and some tinsel to wrap around the bivvy.

Christmas Eve was a dour affair, the temperature had dropped to about freezing and it had become foggy with the high pressure, Kevin Maddocks would have probably packed up and cluttered off home. (See Carp Fever for joke reference). I sat in Rambo's bivvy sipping supermarket brand lager feeling cold, dirty and unloved. It had come to this, unemployed, soon likely to be single, up to my ears in debt which didn't need to be paid back to a bloke who had graduated through the army, then a mercenary and then to an arms dealer who I was fishing with full time on an insignificant puddle trying to win some two-bit contest against the world's greatest shithead. It could have been worse, I could have been fishing with Watt against Rambo, at least the way things were I was unlikely to die which I considered was always a feasible option when you did anything against Rambo.

That night was the closest I came to actually seeing things as I can see them now, it lasted maybe half an hour and then the effects of cheap lager on an empty stomach tipped my mind away from the truth and it never regained that elusive condition until the end of my story. I had returned to TWTT mode as strongly as ever.

Rambo sipped his lager along with me and started to tell me another yarn, something about machine gunning an entire battalion while carving a dug out canoe with a Swiss Army knife with his other hand to make good his escape down the Amazon, Nile or Thames, whatever it was. Then we talked about the syndicate, sex and what car we would buy if we won the lottery. Then we talked about what sex we would try to buy if we won the lottery and then what business we would buy into which brought us back to the syndicate. I guess everyone dreams of owning his own water.

"I tell you what," I said, the effects of the lager now evident.
"What?" Said Rambo.
"I wouldn't let Watt fish it. I'd let him be in charge of dog turd reclamation, though."
"You wouldn't want dogs around a lake that you owned, would you?" Asked Rambo.
"I bloody would if Watt was in charge of clearing the dog muck. I'd have the biggest dogs money could buy. Great Danes, Rottweilers, St. Bernard's........can't think of any more.....and I'd over feed them."

I then collapsed into hysterical laughter. (Incidentally Rambo must be thanked for this part of my tale because I can't remember hardly any of it, he can handle his drink better than me). I carried on rambling about Watt for a while and then got back on to the subject of fishing and then somehow onto the subject of fishing and music and songs that could have their title changed slightly so that they were fishing related. I list a top ten that came out of my hyper-active mouth as a bit of fun for you. It is a stern reminder of how addled you can become when constantly fishing and when it's Christmas Eve in the bivvy and 3.5% proof lager has had a go at you. I suppose you need to know the real song title to get the joke but I'm sure that amongst yourselves there will be enough diverse musical tastes to get them all, so here goes; Tainted Bait - Soft Cell, Strawberry Cream Forever - Beatles, Reeling in the Carp - Steely Dan, Smells like Tutti-Frutti - Nirvana, I don't like Blanking - Boomtown Rats, Tiger Nuts - Mud, Down at the Gravel Pit at Midnight - Jam, Casting in the Dark - Bruce Springsteen, Hooks, Hooks, Hooks - Sparks and Potassium Sorbate - Suede. Ok, sad. Fair comment.

After this Rambo hinted that he wanted to get some kip and who could blame him.
"Not going to walk me home then?" I giggled.
"Out the bivvy, turn left, walk five yards, turn left again. Home. Don't forget the first turn left bit because I'm not going to pull you out the lake and you'll probably drown."
"Merry Christmas," I said but my mind kept saying 'turn left, turn left'.

I scrambled safely into my bivvy, nearly leapt through the top of it as a bit of tinsel tickled the back of my neck and then collapsed on my bedchair. The morning came and I awoke with a mild headache to a bright, crisp Christmas Day. Four hours later a snappily dressed Kipper rolled up with wellies over his nice trousers and walked down to the Big Pads. My guts turned and not because of the cheap lager, Maddocks was wrong, one of them had had a twenty in the night. In due course, as it was my turn, I moped down to the Deep Corner to meet Kipper who was standing with a fish in a weigh sling. Without a word he handed me the sack and Mike's scales, I put the scale's hook through the two metal triangles of the weigh slings chords and held it up. A cursory glance, well into the 22's. I nodded. He nodded back. I watched him go to the scoreboard and take off the protective layer of plastic sheeting. One last hope to make it a bit better. Rats! Kipper wiped out the 17 and made it 18, Watt had caught the fish. Or had he?

Although everything was as watertight as possible, at night it was impossible to know who had caught the fish, we just hoped that Harry still had enough interest not to pass on the odd twenty to Watt. I couldn't see him being that subordinate to go to the massive step of fishing full time and then giving his rewards to Watt. But who really knew after all that had gone on before, all those early season revelations spinning off one after the other, who would have imagined them? As Kipper walked off towards Watt and Harry the scoreboard told the truth even if it was lies. The scoreboard was the log book ... was the decider of the winner of the TWTT. Christmas. Bah! Humbug!

The lake was fairly busy from the day after Boxing Day until New Years Eve because most of the rest of the syndicate were on holiday. Dave and Tony turned up early one morning and decided to fish the Deep Corner. It was quite amusing to watch the pair of them from a distance, you didn't need to hear their conversation only to observe their body language. The odd frustrated arm was thrown in the direction of myself and Rambo and also (gasps from the audience) at Watt and Harry. As each runless second advanced so Dave became more exasperated and by midday it was time for the two sets of protagonists to rub salt in an ever widening wound. Rambo had a low double and an hour later Harry landed what looked to be a smallish common. Both Dave and Tony were pacing around their apparently useless swim like caged tigers, they knew that they weren't in the right spot but the poor bastards were unaware that they also weren't on the right bait as Watt had neglected to pass on the secrets of our boilie.

Eventually about half an hour after Harry's fish Dave's patience snapped and he stomped back up towards the pair of us. I wondered what was about to happen as I hadn't uttered so much as a single syllable to him or him to me since our little clash over his lost fish.

"Are you fishing in this swim until March?" He asked brusquely.

Here we go, I thought. "Yep, we sure are." I said with the total confidence of a man whose fishing partner standing not six yards away was capable of pulping and rendering unconscious an alligator who had had the benefit of a six month course of steroids and a personal fitness instructor.

"And are Watt and Harry going to fish the Big Pads all that time as well?"

"I don't know what they're going to do, why don't you ask them?"

"Bloody great for the rest of us, having the two best swims wiped out for the rest of the season."

I shrugged my shoulders and looked away at my Delkims. I felt like saying that I probably needed to fish until July to make up the rod hours what with Dave and Tony fishing six a piece at times, I didn't though because I knew it was too wild an exaggeration to make it stick. Instead I just said, "there's nothing in the rules about how long you can be in a swim after the first day draw week."

"I see Watt's catching you up," Dave said trying a new tack.

"Phh. A bit," I said as if it was the least important thing in the world rather than the most and then rather maliciously I added, "of course he should, having pilfered our bait. That's why Harry and Mike have started to catch more as well. I notice you Tony and Kipper got bugger all out of it, I expect Watt was worried that you two could win the TWTT. You know the pair of you catching four fish thirty times each."

I was really pushing the boat out here but I could sense Rambo (alligator crusher by Royal Appointment) starting to walk over. The reason I could sense this was that Dave's eyes had looked up to see Rambo coming his way and his skin had paled to ghostly white. I now knew why people bought and kept rabid Rottweilers.

"What are you trying to say? What do you mean your bait was nicked? What do you mean four fish thirty times?" He blurted incoherently.

"Nothing. Ask Tencher. Repeat captures generally mean that you do have to catch the fish repeatedly. There, does that answer your questions?" I said eloquently as Rambo appeared at my shoulder.

Dave looked at me with bewilderment and then at Rambo and comprehension dawned on him, time to push off before Rambo got involved. He turned and went back to Tony and the Deep Corner where the pair of them had an animated conversation before Dave walked around to where Tencher was fishing and then back to Watt. God knows what bullshit the pair of them told him but it must have reminded Dave of how he had felt about Watt and Co before he had become a turn-coat and sided with them just because I had inadvertently failed to net a certain twenty for him. He also must know that his pathetic little scam of photographing fish that either him or Tony had caught in different swims wearing different clothing had been rumbled. I was feeling pretty proud of the mental turmoil he must have been experiencing. That'd teach him to go crawling to the enemy.

The holiday week moved on while the fishing stayed put. As luck would have it the lake fished poorly after the two fish out on the day after Boxing Day and not one fish came out until New Years Eve when all the others apart from the four full timers had gone home. Shame for them wasting their valuable holiday like that! I caught the common that ended the long period of inactivity but it wasn't a log book common, in fact none of the commons were, the largest so far was only thirteen pound or so.

That New Years Eve, Sophie of all people turned up, tip toeing her way by torch light to find me wrapped up in my sleeping bag in the bivvy. It was about ten-ish when she poked her head around the door opening and shone the torch in my eyes. I had no idea who it was because I was dazzled by the torch light but she was the last person I expected, apart from Dick Walker but then he's dead. We had a strained conversation about how things had gone at Christmas, how the family was and all that sort of thing and what she was doing to celebrate the New Year.

"I've come to see you to do that," she said softly and snuggled up to me on the bedchair. I briefly wondered if she'd been at the Archers but there was no smell of peach.

"That's nice," I said. To be honest I was amazed that she could be like that to me after all that had happened. She then explained to me how she could.

"When this is all over, we will get back to normal won't we? You know you'll get a job and we'll actually have a life together?" She said quietly.

For a minute I felt as if I was in some film where I was a pilot who had briefly met his fiancè before he had to go back to the war. That damn war. The next thing was that I realised how she had decided to deal with our situation. A lot of girls would have told me to ship out but Sophie now thought she could cope with it if it was only a temporary aberration, albeit nine months, provided there was light at the end of the tunnel. We weren't going under because Rambo was paying the mortgage, it was just time out. I had no desires after having seen off Watt.

"Of course. When this seasons over I'll be free to get back to normality. " The massive irony of that statement. (See later). "I know this has all got a bit heavy and I know that I've become a bit possessed but it's just something I've got to do. When it's over things will be fine."

"Promise."

"Promise." I said and leaned over to kiss her. She kissed me back.

I might get to see the New Year in with a bang so to speak I thought. Wah-hay I'd never done it in a bivvy. We snuggled closer, she breathed hotly into my ear. No sooner had her breathe started to chill when it was displaced by 80 odd decibel's worth of screaming high tone Delkim sound wave. I scrambled out quickly not heroically to a nearby Spitfire as in my film but to a twelve foot carbon carp rod where I fought a rather one sided dual with a seven pound common that had Christmas torpor rather than an ace Meschershmidt pilot. Not surprisingly the ambience was shattered and Sophie muttered a 'think I better go now' speech. We said our goodbyes and she left me alone. I sniffed my fingers after unhooking the carp. Pretty close I thought rather crudely and slumped back on my chair.

Now there will be no prizes for guessing my New Years resolution that night as I sat in the pitch black listening to my radio. It only remains to add that as much as I would have liked to win the TWTT outright I had no competitive feelings against Rambo, my ambition for what it was worth was to blow Tom Ya Man Watt into third place, fourth would be even better if Harry was feeling keen. I saw myself as insurance for our side if for some unknown reason Rambo disappeared off the scene. Alien abduction or an old enemy hit squad seemed about the only possibilities there, I couldn't see his fishing tailing off that badly. I was back up and that was the top and bottom of it, Rambo was the number one driver but the number two driver still had an important job to do. The number two driver still had burning ambition but it was all directed at Tom and Harry, if the truth were known and it came down to it I could survive on Rambo alone stuffing Tom and Harry. The gloat factor would still be there but how much nicer if I could do it as well. I turned off my radio to concentrate and show myself how much I meant it.

Chapter 13

Early January saw the first prolonged spell of cold weather, clear, very frosty nights followed by bright days with the thermometer just hovering around zero. As things had been relatively mild the lake took about four days before it iced over and then the four of us were left in a hideous quandary. To pack up and leave would mean the possible loss of our respective swims so we had to sit it out and wait for the thaw to end our ridiculous plight. Fortunately this spell of nature-enforced stoppage lasted only three days but it was the most bizarre of circumstances to be 'fishing'.

Personally I took on an almost reptilian air, apart from Watt most likely thinking I was a snake, I knew what it was like to feel cold blooded. Without the warmth of the sun to warm my body I, like the rest of the reptile world, lacked the means to move, the cold burrowed into me and my brain iced over. I had fished in colder weather when the wind had dropped the chill factor way below what it was then but the wind, coupled with the fact that at that time I was fishing a large gravel pit had stopped any water surface freeze up. Now, staring out at a frozen lake unable to go home and humanise myself I was sluggish and trapped in a treacle world where the vary nature of its viscousness made motion a slow tedious affair. It was all about motivation, with my rods pulled in and absolutely no chance of a take time stood still. Maybe that had frozen as well.

Those three days were the worst of the whole nine month campaign and seemed to last interminably. I read a book once - Catch 22 - where one of the characters said that time goes more slowly when you're bored. He strived to attain the most boring lifestyle available so that his life seemed longer and therefore gave him more value. In the book he loved shooting skeet because he hated it and it bored him which was what he wanted. I now know that it is true, time does drag when you're bored and every look at the watch that said five minutes when the mind thought half an hour proved it.

At last the weather changed and with it my attitude, as soon as the bombs hit the water I was back in business. The race for the TWTT was back on again. Rambo had been oblivious to any weather related problems like he seemed to be oblivious to most things, only Watt had managed to get under his skin and really get to him. Even on the coldest day Rambo hadn't resorted to a polar suite but he did look even beefier than normal so I guess he had put on a thick jumper under his camouflage jacket. In a way I would have liked a bit of snow at that time just to see if Rambo had a set of white fatigues available to help him in his seemingly lifetime commitment to blend in with nature. You know the type I mean like those skiing Nordic soldiers use. Sadly it was not to be and the snow never came.

January's Carpworld came to the world all right and came to me via Tradders. I eagerly scanned the contents page for Watt's article only to find that it was not there. The old boy hadn't made the deadline or hadn't wanted to because at the time of required supplication he was too far behind to bear writing about it. Now he was catching up I imagined him sitting in his bivvy with a candle on his head for illumination. He had a candle holder that was strapped around his head and under his chin, dew drop on the end of his nose and was furiously scribbling away pausing only to put ointment on the wax burns to his scalp. I could imagine his lurid prose being put down in neat handwriting whose small consistent size was at direct odds to the large, sprawling ego that controlled it.

Unfortunately Watt was now having something to write about, success, his success. Ominously he kept picking up the odd twenty, one in one week one in the next fortnight, one again the week after that. By February the first he had made it to 21 twenties, Rambo had just nudged onto 24 and yours truly was going through the football strikers equivalent of a rather barren patch. Despite playing every match I hadn't scored since the last year. I was resolutely stuck on 20. The real trouble was that I couldn't even reel out the old cliché of saying that I was still creating the chances but just couldn't put them away. I had been runless for three weeks.

I started to worry about where I was fishing. I started to worry about presentation. I started to worry about the bait. Rambo told me to forget it and carry on. Instead I started to worry about how tight I was to the Island, I could have been in too close but then again perhaps I was falling a bit short. My margin casts never seemed just right either and I worried about them. Then I started to get concerned about individual things within the presentation area. Were my hooklengths too short now? Then again they could be a touch long, same with the hair as well. What about hooklength material? Maybe I needed to fine down a bit or maybe go to mono. Perhaps the bomb could be a touch lighter as well. Was the bait right for winter? I asked Rambo if he thought we should start to alter it and he said 'no'. I wondered about how much bait to put in, how many boilies to put on my stringer if I decided to fish with one or would I be better off just fishing a single hookbait and then, where should I cast it? In short I became the round and round in circles, disappear up my own backside carp fisherman I had been before meeting up with Rambo. The one difference was that he told me to shut up grizzling and wait it out. I had been the most successful angler on the water apart from him and had done well in both summer, autumn and winter. He told me it was just one of those things that just happen from time to time and soon fate would put fish my way. Luckily I listened, had I been on my own I would have probably chopped and changed and got in a right state.

At last my nightmare ended, three days into February I at last managed to get off my bogey number of 20. I felt as if my whole life had taken a huge step forward, the trouble was that Watt's results were heaving years off of it. It was clear that Watt's superior fishing ability (OUCH!) coupled with our boilie was making it all very, very dodgy in terms of us sticking it up him. It also seemed that whether by Watt's design i.e. clever baiting and tactics the Big Pads was turning out to be a better swim than our Island swim.

Over the years these two swims had been the best in the summer and autumn months but I would say that everyone in the syndicate given the choice would opt for the Island. It seemed more consistent under differing weather conditions and was always easier to actually land fish than the Pads. You could be much more relaxed about fishing the Island whereas the Pads was a definite, by the rods job all the time. Having said that the inevitable tail off in numbers that winter brings had never really subjected the two best swims to constant pressure as they were seeing now. A direct winter comparison was not available, some had fished the odd weekend where there was a good chance that you might blank in any case and if you're not catching you can't really learn too much. Now with both the Pads and Island under constant six rod attack a more precise analysis could be made. That precise analysis comprised the basic reality that we were in the wrong bloody swim, or I suppose that Watt was fishing the pants off the pair of us. In all honesty I think it was 30% the former and 70% the latter because Harry only kept pace with us where Watt actually hauled in the ground.

It sounds dramatic, 'hauls in the ground', I mean it wasn't like a sprinter running down a geriatric on crutches more like a tortoise running down a snail. What you have to remember is that this is a very condensed version of what happened, a whole month - Pow! - Gone in a paragraph. It would not have made a riveting live programme for Sky Sports..... "well that ends our 48 hour programme from the syndicate lake. Just to recap, nothing happened, no takes, not even a liner. The scores are still the same as they were for the last two shows but well be back in a couple of days time for another 48 hours of uninterrupted coverage". Well let's face it no-one would buy ad time, would they?

Watt's long fight back lacked explosive action but the slow insidious nature of it gave me the willies all right.

"Looks like Watt's into another one," Rambo would utter matter of factly and I would look with genuine pain at the bend of his rod which seemingly parodied the downturned expression of my mouth.

Then of course sometime later, the waiting was terrible, either myself or Rambo would or wouldn't be called down to no-man's land to witness the twenty if that indeed was what the fish had been. A couple of times I was convinced that we had got away with it and the latest fish had only been a double but there was obviously some delay in getting the third party to the lake and once they had turned up we knew the scoreboard would have to change once more.

Watt and Harry must have had a mobile phone like we had and I sometimes wished that I knew their number so that I could give them some horrendous abuse down the phone. I had been told that apparently the 1471 number didn't work on mobiles so with voice disguise I would have been safe, but I didn't know their number so that was the end of that. During my three week blank I wondered whether I knew anything, Rambo assured me that I still knew how to be a pain in the arse and he was probably right

The slow drip, drip, drip of twenties falling to Watt's rods was like Chinese water torture to me. Rambo remained unfussed on the surface, he certainly wasn't falling apart like I was because his catch rate had dropped, but I knew how much this meant to him and he knew I knew. By the opening day of March Rambo had 25 twenties to his name, Watt had 23, Harry had 16 and I had 22, perhaps more importantly since Christmas Rambo had caught just two twenties and after all my whinging I had caught the same, as had Harry, but Watt had caught five. My actual fish catch had been down on everyone else after my three week runless hell but I had fluked out of it by catching the bigger fish.

"Jesus, this is all getting a bit close for comfort," I said to Rambo with heavy despair. I was feeling low as I had just had to bare witness to a grinning Mike that the fish he had handed me and that I was weighing was the fish that let Watt tread on my head like a stepping stone to take over second place.

"Sure is," said Rambo, "so get your finger out and start making it more roomy. If I die in my sleep tonight you're all that can stand between Watt and the TWTT. I need your support Matt, you never know what might happen, you're still very much part of the plot, boy."

Rambo gave me a playful punch on the shoulder that nearly flattened me, it felt like the recoil on twenty shotguns taped together and fired at once. (That's funny looking at that sentence, I can remember thinking it at the time for some abstract reason, but why twenty shotguns, it could have been any number ten, thirty or twenty-five. Of course you don't have to be Freud to answer that one, Twenty was the number my brain was tuned to). His little pep talk worked and boosted me up a bit but I was at odds as to how to manifest this new enthusiasm. That old chestnut is the perennial problem with fishing, just how do you try harder? The normal answer is to fish more and longer but as I was fishing 100% of my time I was stumped on that front. I certainly saw little room for new tactics and experimentation either. Not the kind of ridiculous change for change sake panic induced groping I had considered earlier but the kind of methodical, straight thinking ideas that can produce bonus fish. The trouble was that I was scared of it backfiring. We were now at the 80th minute of the World Cup Final and I revealed myself to be a sad indictment of the English game, plodding on with little imagination, long ball oriented, frightened of reasoned change and unwilling to try it. The only fact that was at odds with my analogy was that I had been very successful recently and didn't have to go back to 1990 for competence or 1966 for genuine success.

I wondered how Watt had managed to increase his twenty catch rate and once again Rambo seemed to think clearly on the subject. "Well, we must assume that they are on identical rigs and bait and as far as I can see with the old binoculars they both seem to be employing the same tactics."

"So why is dog's breath catching more?" I said somewhat annoyed.

"Well, he doesn't seem to be picking them off from any one particular spot, his takes, the ones that we have seen during the day seem fairly evenly spread across his rods. I'm sure that he isn't doing anything that much different from us because if he had been I'd have been having a go at it. The other thing is that I'm convinced that Watt would have persuaded Harry to come in with him full time so I can't see even Watt being able or wanting to hide anything from Harry and yet he's out catching Harry to about the same extent that he is out catching us." Rambo paused to shrug and screw his nose up.

"So what are you saying, then?" I said.

"I'm saying that unfortunately that indefinable knack, that unfathomable ability to winkle out carp here and there when others can't and to carry on doing it when others can is finally making itself felt. This mysterious factor had been held at bay by our superior boilie but after the dustbin affair that has long gone. In short, and though it galls me to say it, the viewpoint always held within the syndicate that Watt was the best fisherman amongst us appears to be true. It seems that given roughly equal time, equipment, bait and similar swims Watt would catch more than me or you. We were lucky enough to have a good start on him, whether it will be good enough remains to be seen."

"Oh shit!" I said with feeling. "Why didn't we have a mini ice age instead of a three day freeze up."

"What up till midnight March 14th?"

"Yeah. We'd have won then all right."

"We may still win," said Rambo. "I'm still in the lead buddy-boy and I have no intention of letting that conniving git get his mits on that trophy."

And so on we went. The rest of the syndicate hadn't been around a great deal during January and February but as the weather started to get milder and we broke into March the 'last chance before the (then) close season' mentality started to rear its ugly head. The head was ugly because that was the general attitude towards us four swim hugging pro-carpers. Watts original achievement in siding the rest of the lads, apart from Tradders, well and truly against us had been all but forgotten as time had eroded that particular avenue of thought. I suppose it made little difference to myself and Rambo, we were still unpopular and that was all there was to it but Watt and Harry made unlikely passengers in the same boat. So it was that the lake became much busier and feedback eventually started to er.... feedback to us. The general consensus was that the TWTT had been a fair idea given normal fishing practices, however the ridiculous lengths that the four of us had gone to had rendered the whole thing crazy. I had to laugh at this when Tradders told me, one because the real lengths that people had gone to, the snide nasty ones as opposed to the full time fishing that had so griped everyone were still unknown to most. There was also the hypocrisy of Dave and Tony the main whiners who had also had a fair go at some rather unsavoury tactics before they found out that even at the zenith of their cheating they were unable to catch us up and had given it up as a bad job.

As the season entered into its last week the tension had risen to snapping point. The reasons were quite clear, Rambo and Watt were locked at a very creditable 26 twenties each and in fact had been so for the last five days. Unfortunately both myself and Harry looked to be out of it, Harry more so than myself who had just 18 big ones where I could just about hover on the edge of being a contender with 24.

Things had been rather nerve racking as Watt fought back but now they seemed insufferable. Every five minutes we would look over at him and no doubt he would do the same to us and you would think - thank fuck, nothing happening - but when it did, when he got a take - nightmare! I would look at Rambo and he would look at me and I would ask how big it looked and he would say it looked, well, not that big but sometimes fish look smaller when they're bigger and bigger when they're smaller and what did I think, and I would say it looked a twenty and he would say - look, don't say that, say it didn't look a twenty - and I would say - look it doesn't matter what I say it is, it'll be what it is even if it looked different. Rambo said he knew but it made him feel better. Rather superstitiously he said that my denial may be able to affect the genuine reality. I knew he was talking bollocks and so did he but what the hell it wouldn't do any harm. We were, after all, desperate men.

From that time every time Watt had a take the pair of us went through a stupid routine which ended with me saying the words, "no way, Jose, it wasn't a twentay," the strange inflection just to make it rhyme. I would then spin round, face Watt's swim, put my left palm on my right bicep and thrust my right fist up to my nose. It was our voodoo to ward off unwanted twenties. We had started doing it five days ago when Watt had finally levelled Rambo's score.

After this wonderful pageant we would have to wait and see if the magic worked. If Watt released the fish and if we saw that he did, we knew we were safe and could go back to looking at him every five minutes. If we didn't see him release a fish we waited for the dreaded walk to no-man's land knowing our magic had failed. In the end there were so many occasions when we never saw Watt release a fish but it didn't turn out to be a gut churning twenty that I reckoned he was putting them back out of sight just to wind us up. Either that or he had a pile of commons slung around the back of his bivvy.

In the end I made a Watt effigy out of boilies and kept ramming a baiting needle into the one that was his head, ha-ha!.... the biggest boilie I had left. I never once saw Watt collapse in agony or even as much as flap a fly away from his head but it didn't stop me doing it and every time I did I feared for my own sanity. At night all you could do was lie awake and worry about what he might be catching and what the morning might bring and that hideous acknowledgement. On the bright side this hadn't happened for five days, to counterbalance and on the bad side we hadn't made him do it for five days. I was convinced that the longer Watt went without catching the more likely he was to do so soon but perversely the longer we went the less likely we were. My positive charge had drained to earth.

Even Rambo, he of a million night time raids, he of the stuck in a foxhole under mortar attack, he of the live hand grenades in the rucksack was getting the jumps. As we reached the climax he made no attempt to hide his edgy demeanour especially after I had somehow startled him one day when he was away with the fairies and he turned and had me pinned to the floor with a bowie knife at my throat in less time than it took me to say the letter 'R'. I guess it was a bit much to deny it after that. He had apologised profusely, I told him not to worry about it, it was the type of thing that could happen to anyone and could he take the knife off my throat now thank you very much.

It is hard to convey the sense of fear and tension that we were now under, my stomach felt just like the time I had sneaked around the back of Watt's house to catch Mike and Jennifer at it and she had gone to pull the curtains just as I was about to look in. It was like being in Heathrow's departure lounge with a ticket for Oz in your back pocket and you were scared of flying. You weren't actually flying yet but then Watt hadn't caught that twenty that would take him into the lead yet but you get the picture. Every liner put you into orbit, every fish jumping put you into either agony or ecstasy depending on where it took place and every take, well, it was six numbers up in the lottery time, but you didn't know how many winners there would be and were unsure of the prize.

The pressure on the catcher not to lose it was a little less, I felt, than with the poor sap on the net and of course when it really mattered I was on the net. In the last five days I had been on the net three times, no mistakes had been made but the log book/scoreboard had been unmoved by them. The fish had all been smaller commons. If Bernard Langer had the yips with his putter I had the heebie-jeebies with the landing net and it didn't matter a toss which way round I put my hands on the landing net handle it still shook.

Coupled with all these seemingly horrendous worries was the tension that the other members brought back with them. They seemed a bloody nuisance, they got in the way, made noise, disrupted our head to head with Watt. Didn't they realise we had enough to deal with without them all coming along and adding another dimension to an already complex situation. The selfish bastards. Even Tradders could sense how wrapped up in the TWTT I was and I gave him as much time and respect as I felt I could. But as the final week went on he came to see me less and less even though he was fishing all week, basically he left me to my worries.

Another side show could well have been how quickly Dave and Tony would have come over and beat the crap out of me after my accusations some while ago about their blatant cheating. It was like being fourteen again with those nasty big boys who kept coming around and borrowing your tackle and threatening you only at the moment I was with my 'Dad' and they wouldn't dare touch me. All they could do was give me the eyeball and I smiled back. If Rambo ever left the syndicate I would have to get myself a pet Rottweiler to take fishing with me. He would be insurance and he'd have a head the size of a basketball and stuffed full of teeth. The only command he'd know would be 'kill', and maybe if I was feeling benevolent 'mutilate'.

The pressure cooker was full of water and the gas was cranked up. The question was, what was going to make the safety valve think - bugger this, I'm going to jam up. There may have been a chance that there would have been nothing that could have caused it as an individual item but as you know there were many nasty little ones. The final contributing factor was not some hideous deed but something quite mundane. As fate would have it the final day of the season was a Saturday and all the jolly members of the syndicate decided to turn up and fish that last day. Why? Was it the natural desire to have a last go or was it something more sinister and macabre?

Word had got around about the close run contest that was still all square. Unbelievably Rambo and Watt were locked together all square on 26 and I had caught a twenty on the previous Wednesday to put me up to 25. Word had also got around about the tension that was lakeside. Despite themselves and despite their resentment I can only imagine that the rest of the syndicate were somehow intrigued at our situation. I think that the closest approximation as to the reasons why they all turned up to become embroiled in the grisly last rites is something akin to the crowd that goes to see some dare-devil perform a dangerous stunt. In the back of that crowds collective mind is the horrid notion that perhaps something could go wrong, that blood and guts might be spilt and an orgy of destruction would be unveiled before their very eyes, as they were there. Not on telly, not on video but there, in reality right before them and they could say for years to come that they witnessed it as it happened.

How tempting that must be especially when you personally could have a real relevance on what might happen because of what you knew and what you could say or do. That Saturday will haunt me until my dying day with a mixture of horror, laughter and complete incredulity. If only I'd pleaded insanity, albeit temporary.

Chapter 14

Saturday, March 14th. The final day of the TWTT contest. The scores; Rambo 26, Watt 26, me 25, the rest nowhere. Weather; mild and overcast, south-westerly wind, prospects good. All members of the syndicate present, general feeling of more axes to grind than a professional lumberjack who doesn't like chain saws. The tension? Something akin to a cable car hawser at the 'failed weight watchers up the mountain annual dinner' .... on the way down. Chances of a 'Disney style' happy ending? About the same as reading any carp mag cover to cover without seeing a single bait ad.

Dawn had passed over two hours ago and I knew I was alive and kicking. This was quite simply because my heart was banging so loud I could hear and feel it thumping out a deafening rhythm of life. I just hoped it wouldn't collapse over the drum kit. At ten a.m. I noticed that I was developing a nervous tick under my eye, I glanced over at Watt who was sitting on his bedchair. He wasn't sitting on his bedchair like you would do normally, you know, relaxed leaning back, feet up. Oh no. He had folded the bottom half of his bedchair back to make it like a chair and was sitting right on the very edge of it, body doubled up and leaning forward, forearms resting on his knees. He stared forward at his indicators, closer observation showed his right hand edged towards his rods. He was a gunfighter ready to draw. He probably had a pair of starting blocks hammered into the ground with banksticks to help him as well.

My eye fluttered and I shut it, I squeezed harder at an invisible monocle and then opened it. It fluttered even more. I massaged my eyes with my fingertips and looked over to Rambo who was pacing up and down like a caged lion behind his three rod set up. I stared at him and then down to his boots. Momentarily I panicked, he had no boots on, come to that he had no feet to put boots on. He was walking up and down on stumps, four yards this way, turn, four yards that way, turn, four yards this way – ad infinitum. I shut my eyes again, looked away and then looked back and giggled to myself, he had worn away a little trench, just deep enough to hide his boots, by his constant to-ing and fro-ing. Even the strain was showing on him.

Almost at once both eyes started to flutter. I held out my right arm straight in front of me, shut my flickering left eye and moved my head to look down my arm with my right eye. I focused on my hand. My fingers danced up and down, the puppeteer who held the five strings to my digits was heaving and tugging but with no game plan. I put my arm down and wondered if I had St Vitus dance and then suddenly thought.... WATT! I quickly looked over to see if the bastard was into one. He was the same statue as the last time I looked. I took out his boilie effigy and rammed the baiting needle viciously into the oversized pop-up that was his head.

Watt never moved, I sadistically ground the needle around, my face distorted with hate. Nothing. Watt's concentration was unbroken and my eyes were fluttering so much they were beginning to water. It was all kind of getting to me.

In an attempt to divert myself from the pressure I went to make myself a cuppa. My lighter became the most complex implement in the history of man as I tried to wield the flint wheel with a hand that looked normal but said 'boxing glove clad' to my brain's manipulation department.

A dread crept over me, what if I got a run? My body was so screwed up with tension that I seemed incapable of nearly any slightly taxing manoeuvre. Picking my nose seemed big time, playing and landing a carp was the physical equivalent of running to the moon in a pair of borrowed trainers and shorts that chaffed. Talk about getting the elbow, I had the wrist, shoulder, neck, hip, knee and ankle. At last I managed to light my stove and eventually make a cup of tea. If only I had Valium to put in it instead of sugar.

I sat down on my bedchair and saw a sight that both filled me with horror and awe, there over the far side of the lake at barely 10.30 am was Kipper.....fully awake and by the looks of it capable of inter-action with the rest of the sentient world. This fact alone underlined how excited a situation the ten of us found ourselves. I felt even more nervous although I wouldn't have thought it possible.

The morning wore on but the high anxiety never wore off. I don't think I spoke a word to Rambo that morning, it had all been said and the occasional glance was enough to get our thoughts across. They were hardly complex, 'great Watt hasn't had one. Shit nor have we,' would have covered it. I wondered how other sportsmen or women coped with moments of competitive stress, the chances were they were too involved in the physical effort of maintaining what they were doing to mull over the ins and outs of a cat's arsehole like I was with so much time to do so.

This is yet another example of fishing's individual quirks, all that time waiting and when what you're waiting for does happen all the excitement and pent up frustration is over and done with in what? A few minutes? Remind you of something, boys? However, I prayed for that something, The Run, but the expectancy of it and how I would deal with it in my mentally crippled state made me think that it would be better if maybe it didn't happen. Then I chastised myself, I hadn't fought all this way to wimp out at the final hurdle, surely? No! I must be strong and with that I think my whole body started to shake, the tea certainly became a bit choppy - a storm in a teacup, well, mug anyway.

At just after twelve it did happen. I had just looked over at Watt to check that when I had checked thirty seconds earlier I had been right in seeing the old git transfixed in the same position he had been all morning (great bladder control, unlike Harry), when the optonic banshee'd. Middle rod, belter, baitrunner whirring. Me, heart belting, guts churning. Blindly I scrambled to my rod, a little man right at the back of my head said – Calm. Keep calm, no panic – in dulcet tones while the rest of the million multitude screamed - RUN! TAKE! HIT IT! GET DOWN TO THAT

ROD! TWENTY! NUMBER 26! SHIFT YOUR ARSE FAT, BOY! QUICK! DON'T LOSE IT! - But not all at the same time. The next thing that I could really remember was Rambo appearing at my side with the net and I had a rod bent double in my hands.

"Good luck, mate. We need this one," he said to me. His words steeled me and my legs changed from jelly to very thick, cold porridge.

Just to dive off at a tangent at this moment I would like to pose a hypothetical question. Why do we fish for carp, as a particular species? For the different types of methods and tactics we can use? Yeah. Size? Yes again. For its fighting qualities? Definitely. So why is it that when your into a big carp you want it to come in safely and easily with about as much resistance as a doped gudgeon? Especially after you've caught a glimpse of it and seen how big it is? That's two hypothetical questions but never mind. If you've seen that it's a nine pound common thrashing around in the margins you laugh and say great fight, transpose that common to a P.B or lake best mirror or, as in my case a certain twenty it's a different story. Every lunge it makes gives you a near coronary. Maybe as you catch more you lose this fear but then again I expect it's just a case of finding the fish size that freaks you as an individual. Ok, that's all and back to the story.

In a trance I played the fish with Rambo quietly offering sage advice of the 'rod tip up variety'. I was next to useless and would have certainly fouled up without him talking me through it. I was the passenger in the pilot-less plane and Rambo was ground control. Eventually the fish rolled in front of me and I could see that it was Cyril again, the lakes biggest fish. If I could land him he would be my 26th twenty and a third time capture this year. Cyril, unaware of the larger drama that engulfed him just swam up and down against the weird resistance that he had experienced time and time again that was yanking at his bottom lip. He wasn't about to take sides, only his own, and that meant scrap like hell. The unfeeling (let's hope so, or the animal activists will have us on the list next) bastard wiped years off my life in that ensuing struggle as he gallantly tried to reduce me to a gibbering, tearful wreck that his escape would have made me. Strangely I felt like a fish, albeit in a goldfish bowl, all too well aware of the nine pairs of eyes scrutinising me, the vast majority hoping for a mistake on my part or gremlins in the tackle. I just kept thinking – don't come off, please, don't come off. At last the battle started to go my way, Cyril finally thought, 'sod this for a lark' and turned on his side and Rambo, he of the coaching tongue, faultlessly netted him.

It was all too much for me, euphoria couldn't displace the mass energy drain that I felt. "I've got to go and sit down," I said to Rambo and left him to unhook Cyril and sort things out. Very melodramatic but I was shot away.

Mike came around to witness the fish and weigh him, Rambo took some snaps of me with Cyril and then put him back. As I recovered I became elated that I had pulled through and not messed up as I had thought I would earlier on in the day. I stood by my bivvy a man, I was convinced that if I could make it under that sort of pressure and come out of it like I had, I could handle anything. Boy was I thinking bollocks, Rambo had been the rock.

After recasting the implications of being right back in with an equal chance to win started to dawn on me, however, I was not afforded the luxury or pain of dwelling long on the subject. Not even an hour had passed from my conquering of Cyril when Rambo had a take. Rambo got the fish away from the Island and started getting it back towards him when suddenly and most unexpectedly all went solid.

"What's happened?" I asked, much in the manner of how you answer an unexpected phone-call from a loved one.

Rambo wasn't certain. "Well, it feels like its weeded but none of the others have caught up anything down there so I don't know. Shit! This one could be the winner. Just get the net ready, Matt. I'm going to try and shift it."

'Get the net ready. This one could be the winner.' I remember quaking at those words, I had to return the compliment to my fishing mucker, help him through and net that fish. I was dreading it. Rambo proceeded to try and move the fish but it appeared to be well bedded, despite applying fair amounts of sidestrain from various angles nothing budged.

"Is it still on?" I asked.

"Not sure, I haven't felt any thumps. Everything just feels rock solid. I think I'll back off and give it some slack for a while." Rambo laid off the power and let everything go slack for about a minute. The line stayed perfectly still in the water. It was time for a positive decision and Rambo took it.

"Oh well, no more fannying around, major welly time," he said and took a short hike along the bank, shoved the rod tip as far down into the water as he could and gave it the big heave-ho. Amazingly he gained line and then he let out a whoosh of excitement.

"What's up?" I asked excitedly.

"It's still on! I felt it go slack and then, bang! Back tight again. Feels a bit odd but I don't think there's any muck between me and the fish. Right, come on you snot gobbler out you come!"

I hoped there wasn't anything in the way, I was dubious enough about my having to net this one without the fish coming up with a huge gob of weed around its head or up the line just to make things even more tricky. I stood in trepidation as Rambo bullied the fish in close but as much as he tried he just couldn't get its head up. The water boiled out in front of the pair of us. Five minutes passed. Ten minutes passed, then twenty and no sign of what was making all the water move. By now Mike had turned up sensing a situation of unusual oddness that would allow him to wring some fun from it.

"What you hooked then, Rambo? Nuclear sub?" He asked jovially.

"The winning twenty," said Rambo his concentration unchecked.

"It ought to be a twenty the way it's steaming up and down. Mind you, could be a common with an outboard motor on its back."

I stuck my tongue out and sagged my body. "Don't take up comedy, Mike. You'll starve."

By now it must have been a good half an hour since the original take and the syndicate's collective curiosity had been piqued. Dave and Tony wandered round, Kipper was there and so was Tradders, even Tencher made his way to our swim but kept a bigger distance.

"Good crowd," said Mike, "for a Saturday."

He was cut short from making another pathetic comment by the sight of Rambo's rig tubing breaking surface like Excalibur which brought mute murmurs of excitement. I made ready with the net, I was gripping the bloody thing so tight my knuckles were white, much longer and the odd finger might start to drop off through lack of circulation. Soon she showed and yes, Rambo had swanked right, a twenty, a pretty good bet twenty. Rambo still seemed to have trouble getting the fish ready to land and soon I saw why. I could follow the tubing down to the in-line lead and on with the white flecked braid, straight to the fishes side. The slack and then back tight experience must have been caused by the hook pulling out and fortuitously lodging in the flank. No wonder he couldn't get the fishes head up! At last after nearly 45 minutes the fish had tired right out and Rambo dragged her almost sideways up to the net as I gradually eased it under her and lifted upwards. She disappeared into the mesh.

"Yes!!!" I screamed at Rambo.

"Whooohoow!!" He hollered back and we slapped hands like basketball pro's.

After we had put her on the unhooking mat I was clench fisting it all over the place as Mike came over with the rest of them. This must be the winning goal I thought. We'd done it! We'd beaten Watt, surely he wouldn't catch an equaliser now.

"Weigh in number 27 for my old mate, will ya?" I swaggered. "I know a twenty when I see one and to quote John Cleese, I'm looking at one right now" (Dead Parrot Sketch).

Mike knelt down and lifted the mesh away from the fish. "Well, I'll weigh it if you like but I can't see much point. This fish won't count for the TWTT, it's been foul hooked."

"What the fuck are you talking about?" I said unable to believe my ears.

"Look where the hook is," said Mike.

"Well you just look at that," said Rambo pointing to the fresh tear in the fishes mouth that was on the same side as the hook. "That's your original hooking point you moron and its just torn out and lodged where it is now. Any cretin can see that."

"That's most likely an old tear," said Mike. He shrugged his shoulders and continued, "anyway I'm not going to argue with you, I'll get Tom and Harry over to see what they think."

"Oh, like they're going to give an honest opinion on it obviously," I said sarcastically and full of anger.

"Of course they will," said Mike and went to get the pair of them.

While he was gone the rest of them all had a look and murmured and mumbled amongst themselves. Watt, Harry and Mike soon returned, it seemed strange seeing Watt close up. All those weeks in his presence and his in ours and yet no contact other than binocular voyeurism to see what each other was up to. Now I was up close I felt like smashing his face in, the cheating git.

Watt examined the fish saying nothing. After he had looked Harry had a close inspection and then the pair of them had a quick private conversation.

Watt brushed his trousers down and said definitively, "yes we're both in agreement, not too much doubt really. The fish was definitely foul hooked."

"You stupid prick," I said beside myself with anger. "What a surprise to find that you're still a cheating bastard."

"I must say Tom, that is a very unfeasible decision you've made taking in mind the circumstances of capture and the visual evidence, come to that," said Tradders. My heart leapt out to him. What a decent guy.

Watt was externally unruffled "When you have caught as much as what I have, Ian, I think you'll be in a better position to judge these matters," his egometer well into the red line.

"Crap! We think that it was a genuine take and a hook slip and you're just shit scared of loosing. Don't we Dave," Tony suddenly blurted. I was amazed that he had come out on our side.

"Yep," confirmed Dave.

"Huh. Hardly," said Watt but I could tell that he was as shocked as I was at the pair of them siding with us. In his own heart of hearts he must have known that he was trying to pull a fast one and was relying on his position within the syndicate to get him through. Luckily for us it wasn't working out that way.

Harry tried to see the bluff through. "What do you couple of Noddies know about anything anyway?"

"Well, we know that any man that asks me to snoop around somebody's dustbin looking for bait clues must be shit scared of losing," continued Dave not to be put down.

"Especially when they get somebody else to nick the boilie off the hair after a fish has been caught with it." I chimed in, scowling at Tencher.

"And then don't tell anyone else about it but keep it to themselves," said Tony referring to how he and Dave had not been put on our bait..

"And cheat at the first day draw as well," said Dave.

"And prebait," I added cleverly keeping up the attack on things that Watt, Harry and Mike had all done together. "Of course, what really gets me is that we're all paying too much for all this. Not only are we being ripped off one way we're being ripped off another by Mr. Wonderful here," I nodded at Watt, "by paying the farmer less than what he's telling us and pocketing the rest. Along with his buddy, Kipper."

Major astoundment and complete silence

"Do what?" Said Harry.

"He's lying," said Watt calmly.

"Am I? Tell me if I'm lying." I asked Kipper staring him in the eye. Kipper held my gaze for just a second and turned away to look at the tops of his boots.

"I'm.....I'm sorry lads. I was short of money. It was Tom's idea," Kipper blurted. He obviously never had the stomach to try and front people out when it came to the crunch like Watt had.

"You unbelievable bastard," said Dave and started to square up to Watt. Mike quickly stepped in between them.

"For God's sake don't let him kill Watt will you Mike. After all you want your fancy lady but not full time. What with you already having a wife of your own," I said.

"What?" Said Watt. It was his turn to be as dumbstruck as Harry had been.

I went for the jugular. "He's been knocking your wife off for months, you idiot. Why do you think he never fished when you did before you started up full time? Because he was around screwing with your Jennifer that's why."

Watt's face turned to thunder, he stared at me and then at Mike. "You disgusting lowlife. How dare you?" And then believe it or not he swung a haymaker at me! Talk about shooting the messenger. I ducked out the way to see Tony shove Kipper over and Dave swing a kick at Harry.

"For Heaven's sake, are you all out of your minds?" Screamed Tradders.

It was a question that didn't need asking. Of course we were. The ensuing melee was almost slapstick. Kipper flat on his back wallowing in the mud with Tony standing over him reigning down foul abuse while Harry and Dave tried to Kung Fu each other and failed pretty miserably apart from a couple of schoolboy kicks to thigh and buttocks. Tencher had leapt on Rambo's back and was hitting him around the head with a boilie bag that was half full - don't ask why - in a mission that made the Kamikaze look sound of judgement while Mike had picked up Rambo's 42" net and was trying to jab it in its owners solar plexus. Rambo, despite the frontal landing net attack and rear assault powered forward unflinchingly like in the Curse of the Mummy, took hold of the handle and flicked Mike straight in the drink because the fool never had the presence of mind to let go and thought he could resist. Tencher soon landed on top of him as Rambo plucked him off his shoulders like a father taking off his two year old son and flung him on the syndicate adulterer. Meanwhile I was indulging Watt in a game of British Bulldog and winning. I'm not a fighter but could always run pretty quick and Watt being heavier and nearly twice my age had no chance of catching me. I ran just fast enough to keep out of his way as I wove in and out of the rest of them but not fast enough to unduly daunt him.

"Watt's a dirty cheater, his wife's a right old slapper." I sing-songed childishly to taunt him as I avoided his groping arms. "Come on, Watt. Don't give up you pathetic, miserable creep of a man." He didn't for a while but soon tired and became exhausted. He stopped. He'd had it, his hands were on his knees and he was gasping for air through a drooling mouth.

I was heady with rush of it all. "What's a matter with you, you big fat tosser? Ego deflated now we all know what you are? Come on, let's go out with a bang."

And with that I ran to Rambo's bivvy and got out the two hand grenades that I had earlier discovered. I waved them at Watt as I sprinted around to the Big Pads. When I got there I pulled in his three rods and slung them on his bivvy along with the rest of his gear. Consumed with hatred for the man to the point that I was negligent of my own safety I pulled out both pins from the grenades, lobbed them in the bivvy ran like fun and hit the deck. A massive explosion cracked across the lake and Watt's gear was literally blown to smithereens. I walked back to the other nine, eight of whom were absolutely and totally gobsmacked, one of whom was smiling.

As I looked at them gawping at the crater of destruction and drifting smoke on the water (da da da, da da, da daa) that was formerly Watt's tackle and the Big Pads I started to laugh hysterically. What a sight they all were, Kipper was all covered in mud, Tencher and Mike were wet through and dripping, Rambo was smiling, Harry, Dave and Tony still gripping onto each other frozen in mid-fight, Tradders slack jawed with empty weigh sling limp at his side and Watt. Dear old Watt, still breathless and now tackle-less, eyes out on stalks and his face distorted beyond all human comprehension. It was great. Good job, that image had to sustain me very often and convince me that the consequences of what I had done were worth it.

The silence was enormous, everyone seemed stuck in time unable to move or speak. Eventually Tradders whispered, "I put the fish back while you were all......er......busy. I......didn't want it out of the water......" he rubbed the back of his head "... too long. I'll put your sling back." He slowly did what he said and ambled off, shell-shocked. Despite it all he had still meticulously put the fish in a sling to carry it back to the lake and release it. Amazing really.

Now that the silence had been broken Watt managed to gather what was left of his wits about him. "You've gone too far, Williams. You'll pay for this," he wheezed and with that he turned and walked very slowly and shakily up the path to the car park. The rest of us looked around at each other like complete strangers unable or unknowing what to do next.

"At least you don't have to carry all your gear back. Loser!" I shouted to him but I knew I was on the downward slide from my peak.

"Well, I guess that just about wraps it up for this year, boys," said Rambo. "Work party next month? That hole'll need back filling for a start." No-one laughed, dazed they all just sort of drifted off, packed up and went home without saying a word. It was weird.

"What do you think will happen?" I said to Rambo as I put my rod bag in the van.

He gave me a serious look. "You're in big trouble, mate. I for one am about to disappear for a while during the undoubted rumblings that this will produce. I'm afraid I can't afford to be around when the shit hits the fan."

"You're not niggled with me are you?" I asked.

He laughed. "No, mate. If you want you could disappear with me but I don't think that will help you in your social situation." I nodded. "Look, I'm out of here. I'll be in touch. I can help you from a distance so don't think you're alone. Ok?"

It was the last time I saw him. His words didn't make much sense then but as ever he had predicted the likely outcome of events of which I just wasn't aware.

I went home to an overjoyed Sophie. It lasted the time it took me to tell her what I had done. Now it was the low point I thought I'd had before.

"My God. What have you done?" She kept asking and it slowly dawned on me that it was something very serious indeed. Watt's words started to play heavy on my mind and a nervous sickness spread through me. Two hours later the police came and my world fell apart.

Well I won't bore you with the grim details of my statement to the police, how the others were dragged in to shed their personal light on the whole affair, apart from Rambo of course who could be found nowhere. Nor shall I bother you with the trial and my eventual conviction. To cut a long, dark story short I got sentenced to 18 months in the slammer, a lenient sentence apparently, because of my previous good character of not having so much as a parking ticket. The petty dealings that had brought about my actions were not considered, I was told to plead guilty as there were eight witnesses and my recognition of guilt would help with my sentence along with my previous good character. It was a very quick open and shut case.

Due to this on the wider scale Watt's reputation remained much as it was and it grieved me a bit that his character wasn't dragged through the mud but to be quite honest I was more concerned with the hell that a prison sentence would bring. Only after acclimatising as well as I ever could to prison's hideous regime did I resolve to rubbish him publicly.

After six months I felt as if I could cope enough to start to take an interest in something and I knew exactly what that would be. Watt did write his final article in Carpworld about the TWTT and I regret to say that his ego is fully restored, at least it appears so externally. One can but hope that the events have left him emotionally scarred on the inside. I'm sure they have or at least try to convince myself. Once again he painted a warped and unreal picture that ended with his amazing fightback to secure a three way tie in the TWTT and once again to those 99.999rec.% who didn't know the truth, it was a good read.

However, I decided to set about the true story of the syndicate as I indicated at the very start. Time was something I had plenty of and I intended to use it. So that is what I have done and it only remains for me to tell you of the loose ends. Rambo is still abroad or wherever, he writes, he still pays my mortgage and the police can't find him. Through his network of contacts it was put around the prison that I was to be well treated, a massive boost for me as you can imagine. True to his word he continues to be my benevolent guardian angel. If you ever get to read this Rambo, a million thanks. I hope I can shake your hand and fish with you again someday. Of the others Tencher is alive, unfortunately. Dave and Tony still fish together and

Kipper still sleeps but not as well apparently. Tradders has packed in fishing altogether, a totally disillusioned man. For that I am genuinely sorry. Harry has just gone in for an operation on his prostrate gland, he really was the Piddley Problem man after all. Mike has moved in with Jennifer or rather she has moved in with him after Mike's wife found out about all the goings-on and moved out. Watt is all alone with himself, hopefully a sad and bitter man.

The syndicate itself is no more and few have time for any of the others. We were all nearly friends once. The lake now has another set of blokes to pander to and the fish get caught by different people, I doubt if it makes much odds to them.

Apart from that, that's about it really. I don't want to moralise on what's happened to me, nothing is more galling than the ex-smoker or the person who has found religion who tries to ram their experiences and thoughts down the neck of the unwary punter so I shall refrain from doing so. Enjoy carp fishing is all I shall say and leave the rest for you to decide You may have experienced similar things to myself but not so extreme I am sure. Above all I just hope you get the chance to read the truth that's all, I am still unsure how to get my story to the world but somehow the idea of it being a book and getting it published has much appeal.

Finally I thank Sophie for putting up with all the crazy things I have done in the last year and a half, without her I would have gone under. The fact that she will be waiting for me when I come out makes me fight on and the fact that the recipe for Rambo's boilie will also be waiting helps as well. I know it works on other waters because Rambo has told me, obviously he didn't say where and the letter never has a stamp on it but it's good to know. Still, I guess I won't be going as much as I used too and to be honest I don't think I ever will again, well not unless Sophie lets me! Ahh just in time. Lights out and time to scratch another day off. Cyril might be a thirty in my dreams tonight but to be honest he finds it harder to swim into them than in previous days!

THE END